POSTCARDS FROM ALPHAVILLE

POSTCARDS FROM ALPHAVILLE

Raphael
Rubinstein

Hard Press
2000

Some of these texts have been published previously: "Three Conclusions," "Cuarto 105," "From Two Small Notebooks in Memory of Jean Eustache," "Poste Restante" and "A Cameo" in *Lacanian Ink*; "Too Soon, Too Sad" in *First Intensity*; and "Poste Restante" in a 1991 limited edition with illustrations by Shirley Jaffe (Collectif Generation, Paris).

Thanks to Josefina Ayerza, editor of *Lacanian Ink*, for her continuing support and friendship; to Gervais Jassaud for the invitation into the collaborative realm of Collectif Generation; and to Lee Chapman, the intensely responsive editor of *First Intensity*.

Cover still from Jean-Luc Godard's *Alphaville*, 1965
Cover design by Jonathan Gams & Damian Whittaker
Typeset by Chad Odefey

Published in the United States by Hard Press, Inc.,
a non-profit organization: P.O. Box 184,
West Stockbridge, MA 01266
ISBN 1-889097-35-7
Second Printing

In memory of two great artists whom
I was lucky to have as friends and readers

Norman Bluhm
(1921-1999)

&

George Sugarman
(1912-1999)

"Actually, when I come to think about it, a film like this is a little as if I wanted to write a sociological essay in the form of a novel, and in order to do so had only musical notes at my disposition. Is this cinema? Am I right to go on trying?"

Jean-Luc Godard on *Two or Three Things I Know About Her*

CONTENTS

Cuarto 105 13

Jacques de Mercier, Where Are You? 19

Three Conclusions 27

From Two Small Notebooks
in Memory of Jean Eustache 33

August in Olara 45

Mr. Info. 59

Poste Restante 67

A Godard Scrapbook 75

Too Soon, Too Sad 91

A Lost Profile 101

A Cameo 111

14 Things 117

CUARTO 105

"Why have you spoken of this rather than that?"

— Jean-Paul Sartre

Cuarto 105

It is afternoon and I am sitting in a hotel room in Mexico City. (The first sentence should actually have read: "It was afternoon and I was sitting at a desk in a hotel room in Mexico City," but who wants to split hairs?) My mind seems to be working well, but I am not at all sure in which fashion I should start filling up the page of hotel stationery waiting in front of me. Finally, I select as the subject of my first sentence, my most recent act and I write: "I have just set this cigarette in that ashtray." I then add three variations:

> I have just set this cigarette in this ashtray.
> I have just set that cigarette in that ashtray.
> I have just set that cigarette in this ashtray.

While I am writing these sentences, across the 19th-century park in front of the hotel there is a demonstration in progress. What is important to me about the demonstration is that I choose not to watch it, preferring to stay inside this curtained room, scratching at this page. It, the demonstration, matters to me, but only as an event I choose not to attend, even as a spectator. There is something shameful in my even mentioning it here. I would do much better to mention the book about Sartre I was just reading.

That book about Sartre I was just reading is sitting across the room from this desk. In a treacherous world, one of the few things I am certain of is that this desk will remain this desk as long as I am sitting at it, though later, when I will be across the room reading that book about Sartre, this desk will become that desk, as that book about Sartre will become this book about Sartre. Would it be wrong to conclude from this that the difference between this and that is approximately 15 feet?

In the interval between cigarettes, let us suppose that there are two ashtrays on this table. Although they are separated by no more than a few inches, I would refer to them as "this ashtray" and "that ashtray." In fact, we needn't go to the trouble of supposing a second ashtray — there is one already available across the room. If I wished I could bring it over to this desk and place it next to this ashtray. Note: while I was on the other side of the room getting that ashtray, "this desk" would have become "that desk," "this ashtray" would have become "that ashtray" and "that ashtray" would have become "this ashtray." When I would have placed both ashtrays on this desk, I would have to remain attentive or otherwise risk experiencing a vertiginous exchange of articles between them.

I have lit another cigarette and placed it in the ashtray. I do not know why the object that a moment ago was "this ashtray" has now become "that ashtray." It must have something to do with the cigarette. I take a drag on the cigarette and try to imagine conditions under which this desk could become that desk, without me moving away from it. It would not be sufficient to posit the presence of a second desk in the room. No, what I would have to do would be to gaze at this desk as if it were the first one I had ever seen and say: "why, look at that . . . desk!" (Which reminds me of someone I once knew who often used to refer to books she admired, but wished to distance herself from because they were such obvious objects of admiration (at least I think this was her motive), as "that book by X." For example, she would say, "Have you read that book by William Gass?" and I would instantly know that she was referring to *On Being Blue*, which had just come out.) "This desk" might also become "that desk" were I to include it in a list of the things around me (this ashtray, that pack of cigarettes, these matches, that desk, this page) but this would only be an arbitrary shifting of articles.

I have an appointment to meet someone soon, so I had better start formulating some conclusions. The placement of these articles (this/that, these/those) is generally determined by the object's relative distance from the speaker. We are thus supplied with a basic method of categorizing the world, a method which separates the less intimate from the more intimate, joining us to certain phenomena, dividing us from others. Unexpectedly, the despotic categorization effected through these small words is what makes solidarity possible. Let us suppose, lighting another cigarette, the existence of a book from which the words this and that were excluded. (A helicopter just flew over the hotel.) I suspect that their absence would render the book unbearably impersonal. The author would have to use words like one, the and a. The world would be pushed ever farther away:

This ashtray is made of glass.
That ashtray is made of glass.
The ashtray is made of glass.
An ashtray is made of glass.

(Another helicopter just flew past, very low.) For the people marching on the other side of the 19th-century park, "that demonstration" is "this demonstration." In a few minutes, having demonstrated (I can also use the word for what I'm doing) perhaps nothing more than my own predilection for the sound of the letter T (this, that, cigarette, Sartre), I will have to leave this desk to go meet someone in the hotel bar. There isn't enough time to do anything about the space between this and that. The rules of proximity and distance I follow are laid out as rigidly as the lawns and paths in the park across the street. If, in the process of making a barricade, someone pulled down a tree, I don't think I would know how to refer to it. This tree, that tree, a tree, tree. If a fusillade rang out, I would still complete this sentence. If blood ran, I would still be here, sharing this room with that book about Sartre, that dispersing smoke, that supposed reader, this completed page.

JACQUES DE MERCIER, WHERE ARE YOU?

An old guide book tells me that in the 1930s MacDougal Alley, a block of mews behind the north side of Washington Square, was the only street in New York City still illuminated by gas lamps. Last night I went to a party in one of the quaint, two-story houses that line its cobblestone length. At one point I found myself in a quiet corner where the host was showing off a series of photographs he'd taken at various nightclubs in the early 1980s. In several black-and-white, flash-lit images I noticed, among a group of dissolute-looking people seated on a banquette, a man I recognized as one of my neighbors. He was a strange figure who'd sparked my curiosity for years and I jumped at this chance to discover more about him. Responding to my questioning, the photographer-host said he thought the man was a Marxist filmmaker who had directed — or at least somehow been involved with — a famous European political thriller of the late 1960s. He couldn't remember the name of the film. As he spoke, I experienced a kind of mental gasp. This response to my casual inquiry had opened up a pathway between two distantly separated parts of my life. Marxist filmmaker, European involved with a political thriller of the late '60s — the man in the photograph sounded exactly like the elusive Jacques de Mercier, the film-maker engagé who my friend David and I had fleetingly encountered (and ever since wondered about) when we were teenagers in California. How amazing, I thought, if de Mercier had ended up, all these years later, as my next-door neighbor. And how amazing, also (perhaps even more so), to discover this fact in so haphazard a manner, glancing through some nightclub snapshots in the middle of a party at a stranger's house on MacDougal Alley.

I would usually see my neighbor late at night as I looked out of my fourth-story window onto a scene of deserted streets and hulking industrial buildings. At midnight, he would be talking on the corner pay phone or hailing a cab or walking hurriedly across Canal Street. He was about 50, of stocky build, with a craggy face. Always dressed in black and wearing a wide-brimmed black hat, he reminded me of Fellini. I guess I had been noticing him for about a year before I learned that he was actually living in my building, sharing a loft on the second floor with a much younger woman who appeared only at rare intervals, shockingly thin and pale, also dressed in black. As enigmatic as her companion, she was rumored to be a drug addict who lived in squalor and poverty but was due to one day inherit a large fortune. I don't know about the squalor (I never saw their loft), nor about the drugs or the inheritance, but, thinking back, Mr. Black Hat's frequent use of the pay phone does suggest that they were too poor to afford a phone of their own.

In 1974, when we were both 18, killing time between high school and college, David and I and another friend, Wylie, had shared a house in the hills overlooking the East Bay. Temporarily without jobs or girlfriends, we watched a lot of TV, mostly old movies. One night, on a local station, a nerdy announcer filled the gap between features by interviewing a film director in the Bay Area to make a movie about the recent coup d'etat in Chile. The director, whose name was Jacques de Mercier, spoke not only of his current project but of his past work with such luminaries as Welles, Antonioni and Costa-Gavras. In a moment of decisiveness, unusual for us at the time, David called up the station and asked to speak to the director. When, to David's surprise, he actually got de Mercier on the phone, he offered his services for the film. To David's even greater surprise, de Mercier accepted the offer and gave David an address in Berkeley to report to the next day. He did so and was instantly put to work. The job was unpaid, but that hardly bothered David. In 1974, for anyone of our age and background, the combination of cinema and Chile was irresistible.

Each night my friend returned from Berkeley filled with enthusiasm for his new life in the world of leftist film making. Listening enviously to his accounts, I learned that much of the film had already been shot, in Mexico, and that the crew and cast were in California to film the climatic sequence, the attack on the Presidential Palace. They had found a building in downtown San Francisco that was almost identical to the site in Santiago where Allende had died, rifle in hand, defending

Chilean democracy. (It was of course impossible to make such a film in Chile.) Impressively, de Mercier had won the cooperation of Allende's widow, probably on the strength of his long list of credits. In addition to having worked with some of the greatest names in European cinema, he had been assistant director of two award-winning thrillers that combined box-office success with staunch anti-imperialist, anti-capitalist ideology. Like so many other young viewers, David and I had been inspired and challenged by those films. De Mercier had gone on to make one feature of his own (unfortunately, we had never seen it), and had also authored an important theoretical text on political cinema. Had it not been for his Marxist convictions, we surmised, he would probably be making a big-budget film with certified stars. Instead he chose to work with little money, often using amateurs and volunteers. His cast and crew, David told me, were passionately committed to the project and to de Mercier, although the director was, in the tradition of all great filmmakers, imperious and short-tempered.

David's job was in the prop department, assembling uniforms and gathering suitable guns for the extras who would play Chilean soldiers. As the day of the big shoot approached, David enlisted his friends in the project. Given uniforms and rifles, Wylie and I were to play Chilean soldiers. (Not brilliant casting, I thought, but David assured us that, as de Mercier put it, under a helmet anyone could be a convincing soldier.) The filming began one evening at sunset and lasted all night. In the end, it became a frantic race to get the last scenes in the can before dawn. It was exciting work, despite the long periods of doing nothing, interspersed with still longer periods of doing the same thing over and over again. Throughout the night, de Mercier was an indefatigable source of energy, encouraging, cajoling and threatening his inexperienced actors and production assistants until we were performing like professionals, or so it seemed to me.

David, I remember, was the target of one of the director's angrier outbursts when the fog machine he was operating malfunctioned and, instead of shrouding the scene in dramatic smoke, began to spit specks of foam over the actors. Finally, after being told he was a "hopeless American incompetent," David got the machine working and the scene was shot with the required atmosphere. Despite this mishap, de Mercier was apparently impressed enough with David to offer him, a few days later, a paid position on the production. They had finished their work in California and were immediately leaving for the Caribbean to film the next sequence. After much debate, with Wylie and me, with the people working on the film and with himself, David decided, reluctantly, not to join de Mercier. He would go through with his plan to attend college (he'd already been accepted by a small liberal arts school in New England), though the prospect seemed pretty dull in comparison with working on an international film. This decision wasn't made any easier by de Mercier who chided David for passing up what he called "the opportunity of a lifetime." David admitted to me that he was probably making a big mistake, but said he just couldn't bring himself to leap in to a new and unknown life.

In the year or two that followed, we anxiously waited for the movie to be completed and released. David doubted that he would get any screen credit and I was prepared to be lost on the cutting room floor. A succession of films on Chile appeared, but never de Mercier's. We were disappointed and puzzled. About three years later, now both attending the same college, we happened to hear a lecture by an American film director known for his leftist political documentaries. He seemed a good person to ask about our missing film. Approaching him afterwards, we brought up the subject of de Mercier's Chilean movie. Did he know anything about it or its director? He asked us why we were curious and we told him the story of our brief involvement. As we finished our account, he started to laugh, his large, fleshy frame shaking like a building in an earthquake. When the vibrations had subsided, he told us about our director.

For decades Jacques de Mercier (he doubted that was his real name) had made a career out of unmade films. Some great project would always be in the works, usually a leftist epic of sorts, but not a single scene of it would ever reach the screen. When the shooting was over, instead of moving into the editing phase, de Mercier would simply melt away. When he turned up six months later, he would be driving a brand-new sports car and flaunting a brand-new sexy girlfriend. There was considerable doubt as to whether he even bothered to load film into the camera. In short, he was a con man.

Shaken, but still not wholly convinced by this tale, David and I did some research. We looked up the films de Mercier said he had worked on — something I'm surprised we'd never thought of doing before — and found that his name never appeared in the credits. The theoretical text ("Poetry and Praxis in a Political Cinema") he claimed to have written did exist — it appeared in an anthology we had been assigned in our film theory class — but that was the only trace of his career we could find. It now looked as if David had indeed made the right decision in not going off to the Caribbean.

That was seven years ago. Last night, as I solved the mystery of my neighbor with the black hat, I felt that I had simultaneously stumbled across our missing director. My host's description of my neighbor — a Marxist film-maker who had directed or at least somehow been involved with a certain highly successful film made in Europe in the 1960s — easily fit de Mercier, and, though I couldn't remember too well what the director had looked like (I'd only seen him that one night of shooting, and during the TV interview), my neighbor was not wildly unlike the man I remembered. And, as I thought about it more, this neighborhood (and, indeed, this building) is exactly the kind of place where a con artist like him might end up. It must be him, and it should be simple to confirm. I only need to get a look at a piece of his mail. Or even engage him in conversation. But would he admit to being de Mercier? Perhaps he'd changed his name, taken on a new identity. Maybe confirmation wouldn't be as easy as I'd thought. But it doesn't matter — I'm convinced that it must be him. And to think, I almost didn't go to that party!

Another six years have passed (I mean six years since the night on MacDougal Alley, the day after which I wrote the first lines of this text). Without me really noticing, my Felliniesque neighbor and his girlfriend moved out of the building before I was ever able to find out if he was, in fact, Jacques de Mercier. Such are the buffetings and distractions of life that, after typing out a few pages, I quickly forgot about what had seemed an amazing coincidence. I never even mentioned it to David.

But the story (is this a story?) is not quite over. Last month, as I was walking down Prince Street with my friend and neighbor Frank, a middle-aged woman hailed us. She was trying to get someone in a wheelchair down to the street from the second floor. The elevator in their building was broken. Would we help? After a moment of hesitation, we said we would. Following her up the narrow, dark stairway of a building across the street from the Prince Street post office, we looked up and saw an old man in a wheelchair waiting on a landing. Frank, who was ahead of me, called out to him, "Carlo!" Turning back toward me, he whispered: "You remember Carlo, don't you. He used to live in our building, with that beautiful junkie girl." I looked up at the white-haired, blotchy-faced figure and realized who Frank meant. It was the man I suspected of being Jacques de Mercier.

We almost killed poor Carlo carrying him down the stairs, wheelchair and all. He wasn't in very good shape. One arm was bandaged, his face was covered with sores and he grunted in pain as we bumped down each stair. He showed no sign of recognizing Frank and he didn't utter a single understandable word through the whole process. Once we'd reached the sidewalk, the woman thanked us and wheeled Carlo off (to a hospital, I hoped). Frank and I resumed our walk. Naturally, my old curiosity coming back, I asked Frank about Carlo. He told me he was a filmmaker. My heart beat faster. That he'd made a famous political film in Europe. Could it be? Was this feeble old man Jacques de Mercier under another name? Was I going to find out for certain? Then, as Frank continued to talk about Carlo, the possibility of him being de Mercier began to slip away. It wasn't as rapid as my moment of recognition on MacDougal Alley had been, but it was more certain. First of all, as I could have guessed from his name, Carlo was Italian, whereas de Mercier had been indisputably French. Secondly, the film he'd made — Frank knew its title and told me — was not one of those de Mercier had claimed to have worked on. And nothing else Frank knew about him remotely fit the author of "Poetry and Praxis in a Political Cinema." Within a block I had to relinquish the image of that pathway between two parts of my life, but here at least was another link, leading from my black-hatted neighbor to this old, wheelchair-bound man. It wasn't as grand as the connection I'd just lost, but, then as now, I was thankful for anything that suggested life was something more than a straight line in time, day after night after day.

THREE CONCLUSIONS

If I tell you that these pages began as a poem and only later, when the narrative had grown too cumbersome for its trellis of mere verse, was transposed into prose, will you believe me? It doesn't matter of course; one genesis is like another and whether I am believed is immaterial, and yet that is the way it happened and something makes me want to tell you so.

As the story opens (the poem also began with these words), I am leafing through an old notebook circa 1978. Mozart's *Prague* Symphony is playing on the radio and the window of my room is closed for the first time since June. It is now the last week of August and surprisingly cool. The notebook is about 6 by 8 inches and spiral bound. The cover is yellow and in the lower left hand corner are the words "La Reliure Spirale" printed in black. I stop at a page I recognize as being classroom notes. In the middle of the page (blue ink, my handwriting) I read:

> All are fooled except Dupin
> — they are blinded to
> the evidence/truth/letter

and just below (black ink, another's hand):

> pourquoi pas Dupin??

After a few seconds, I realize that these must be notes taken during a philosophy class I attended in Paris in the autumn of 1978. (What does it say about the learning process that I no longer remember the title of the class, but do remember the professor's name?) The name "Dupin," casting my mind back, must refer to the hero of Poe's story "The Purloined Letter" and our subject that day must have been Lacan's "Seminar on 'The Purloined Letter'."

I light a cigarette, too soon after the last but no matter for this is a critical juncture in my confrontation with this eight-year-old page (as well as with the present page) and I want the enforced pause of smoking, both to savor the moment and to plan my next paragraph. After a few puffs, I set the cigarette in the ashtray and continue.

Someone who shared a first name with the heroine of a popular American series of "books for girls" and a last name with an illustrious French writer of fairy tales is the only one who could have written "pourquoi pas Dupin??" As if my certainty weren't enough, I recognize her handwriting. We must have been sitting next to each other and she must have been reading over my shoulder.

The Mozart has just ended.

We were in our early twenties.

I've turned off the radio.

How would I have responded to her written question, to the urgency of its double question marks? I'm certain that I would not have spoken to her and risked interrupting the class. (Not that I was such a well-behaved student, but the class was held in a very small room with fewer than 10 of us sitting around a single table.) Nor did I take the obvious alternative of giving her an answer in writing since the next note ("The other place: Poe/The other scene: Freud"), in my careful blue printing, has nothing to do with her question. (I've put out the cigarette.) Was I annoyed at her question, annoyed because it distracted me from the evenly cadenced, dauntingly dense sentences issuing relentlessly from the mouth of our brilliant young professor? Or was I flattered by it, by the implication that she believed I would be able to say why Dupin was not fooled? Probably the latter. I doubtless glanced at her briefly, shrugging my shoulders or silently mouthing the words "I'll tell you later," and returned my attention to what the teacher was saying. I wish I knew for sure how I responded to these inconsequential words that have freakily survived until now. Did we sit down somewhere after class and discuss Lacan? Did I know "why not Dupin"? How much did the two of us care?

I am half tempted to answer her question here, to give these pages over to an analysis of Poe's story and Lacan's commentary, except that the moment for such efforts seems long since over. Not only is it too late for me to answer her question (assuming I didn't do so before) but it's also too late for me to summon the rigor necessary to read Lacan, even to believe that I need to read Lacan.

Instead of grappling with Poe and Lacan, I'm thinking of a postcard I have somewhere in the bottom of a box of old papers. It contains an impassioned message from the person who asked "pourquoi pas Dupin??" to her then boyfriend. I would find this postcard and introduce its text into these pages were I not certain that the search for it would be a long one and that at its conclusion I would no longer be interested in finishing this exegesis, at least not today. I don't remember now how I came into possession of that card. Did I "purloin" it? Did she give it to me to deliver by hand when I flew back to New York where its addressee was? And did I then intentionally pocket it as part of some amorous stratagem, or did I simply neglect to carry out her request through sheer negligence? Trying hard to remember, I think she probably left the postcard in my apartment one day, and I probably never got around to returning it to her, or simply didn't notice it, until it seemed too embarrassingly late to give it back.

The poem that I set out to write was going to lead into a metaphoric reading of her question. I never decided how, and now that page of old classroom notes which seemed so promising looks as foreign and mute as a tablet of hieroglyphs. The best I can do is to add some further notes made in the same notebook on the same day. Under the heading "3 conclusions," still using the same blue pen, I wrote:

I. Signifying Chain (trajectory)
displaces the human subject.

II. Man inserts himself in the
chain of a certain number
of signifiers.

III. Only after he has been placed
in this chain, order, is
there a subject.

FROM TWO SMALL NOTE-BOOKS IN MEMORY OF JEAN EUSTACHE

"I like to live among those who have chosen
the same cinema as I have."

— J.E.

The following text, by far the oldest in this book, dates from early 1982, when I was 26. It was written during an 8-month sojourn in San Francisco. Eustache had committed suicide in November 1981. My immediate response to the death of this French director, whose 1973 film La Maman et la Putain *(The Mother and the Whore) I took as an esthetic model and a personal talisman, was to write a short prose poem about him. It was after only losing the page on which I'd scribbled this poem that I began the following text. My fear that I would never regain the inspiration I felt when writing the initial poem may account for some of the stylistic nihilism of these notes, but they also reflect my then-current ambition to write pages that would be like black holes, voids into which everything would disappear, even my own writerly intentions.*

The "two small notebooks" were free samples I'd recently picked up at a print-industry fair. Most of their few pages were filled at the Caffe Puccini on Columbus Avenue, though when I needed a break from the Puccini, which featured large plate-glass windows, a jukebox filled with Italian pop music and an endless drifting in and out of friends and acquaintances, I would cross the street to the much quieter Europa.

After the three-hour-and-forty-minute triumph of La Maman et la Putain, *Eustache made only one other feature,* Mes Petites Amoureuses *(1975). When he committed suicide, his friend Alix Cléo Roubaud wrote, in her journal, of his suicide "as a natural death; as if he had carried death in himself for so long that he had to die."*

It seems so long ago; for all the influence your work has exerted on my life, and despite the now ineradicable subterranean influence which it continues to exert, I cannot help but feel that if I am able to write about the relationship between you (J.E.) and I, it will be as if some kind of inquest were being held over the body of my past.

This has something to do with the fact that I no longer feel so passionate about *La Maman et la Putain*. Not to say that I like or admire the film any less, nor to say that I no longer find its elegiac Parisian ambience infinitely compatible with the particular form of my own real and imaginary existence, nor even to say that I am in the slightest disagreement with the painful purposeless negativity which radiates from its quiet black and white surfaces. No, it is not that the film has lost any of its meaning. No, it is not that I have changed. It is much simpler: I have now lived with it for so many years that it has ceased to possess that degree of mystery, that something more, the pursuit of which engendered within me an obsessive attraction, a fascination, an infatuation which has ebbed away. Leaving what?

Isn't it like an old friendship? Something one takes for granted, an essence which one has absorbed, which one knows.

***

I have decided (almost wrote "resolved" but then remembered that I am not at all the sort of person who has that particular knack) that when writing in this notebook I will do so only in cafés. A partial explanation of this is that these days cafés are practically the only place I feel like writing, but it also so happens that this locus is thoroughly appropriate to my subject.

What I like, one of the things I like, about writing in a café is the possibility of being interrupted at any moment by the appearance of a friend. There are also the more numerous interruptions of acquaintances, those with whom a brief exchange suffices.

It is already four o'clock but I don't feel quite ready to write today.

***

"To speak with the words of others." In the movie Alexandre expresses this desire. I wouldn't mind writing just now with the words of others, say Ponge or Roussel.

***

It so happens that at this moment I am taking great recourse in the figure of Alexandre. Like me he "does nothing," has never done anything.

He spends his days reading and writing in cafés, his nights meeting girls, wandering the city. He is surrounded by those who do do things, whose lives are more regular than his and in relation to whom he feels at once superior and impotent. In short: not the kind of guy any girl wants to marry.

***

There is something J.E. addresses himself to, represents constantly, which is definitely absent in Ponge or Roussel, or if it is there it can only be reached by extreme extrapolation. I am not sure exactly what to call this.

I have waited long enough for my friends. I will leave and come back later, hoping to find them waiting for me.

***

Something odd is happening. I am not sure how to write about it, or even if I should. It is not part of my subject proper and yet it is inextricably attached to it.

Now I suppose I've got to tell a story, having set the stage for one.

***

The last time I saw *La Maman* I went with a group of people, several of whom had not seen the film before. They all liked it but two, both women, reacted with disgust to the characters portrayed. They found them boring and inhuman, complained that they never smiled, never did anything except drink, talk, go to cafés and make love. One of the women was French and said that she had known people like that in Paris (and that she didn't like them then and still didn't like them now, even in a movie).

I enclosed the last part of that sentence in parentheses because I don't actually remember my friend expressing those feelings, but she easily could have.

The reaction of my friends shocked me. It had never dawned on me that there was the slightest thing wrong with or detestable about those characters!

***

Night is coming on. At a certain level, an imaginary objectivity, a bird's-eye view, I can see how my writing is the act of a drowning man trying to save himself by grabbing hold of mere water. The only difference is that in my case it works.

I feel I am writing without ambition, without style, without a single redeeming and entertaining quality: mere exercise.

***

He is the only one before whom I can stand and be understood. The attempts of my "friends" to "understand" I can only think ludicrous.

***

I think it is time I stop fooling around and begin to work directly on a text for and about Eustache. In order to do so I must first decide whether I want to return to the development of the metaphor of the ashtray which figured in the first note I made after hearing of his death. All that I'm writing now is to make up for having lost that scrap of paper.

Perhaps I could start with a list of themes:
suicide
the aftermath of May '68
café life
the dynamics of sexual triads
the collective philosophical impact of French cinema
Paris as the Universe

***

I just thought of the scene where Alexandre and his friends are in a café and see Sartre across the room. They describe how he is always drunk but manages to conceal the amount of wine he consumes by only ordering half bottles.

Another small thing sticks in my mind. I wonder if it is important or not. Veronika always says "down by the water" when she talks of the Seine. At one point Alexandre calls attention to this quirk of hers and laughs at it.

***

As I write more without having yet begun, without having engaged my subject — the way one engages the gears in a car and then shoots steadily ahead — things become somewhat more complicated. Nonetheless, there are a couple of things which I have just become aware of: 1. I am beginning to want to write about other subjects, and this is a reason for joy, not because I don't want to write about Eustache (who I have not yet begun writing about) but because it means that there actually may be something inside me. 2. This small notebook, which I picked at as a free sample at a printing fair, will not be long enough. I have already reached the last page.

***

It sometimes seems likely to me that there is no such thing as a subject. I first entertained this suspicion because it is a perennial difficulty for me to stick-to-the-subject-at-hand. Actually, it is much worse than that. My weakness (n.b. that if I were speaking I would give this word an ironic inflection) is not that I tend to stray from the subject but that I tend to have no subject at all.

I have begun the second notebook. I am in a café (of course) and the sun is shining brightly down on the table, the coffee, this page and on me (and this bright sun is not an "of course" but a gift over which I have no control. Not true: although I have no choice about whether or not the sun shines, I do have a choice over whether I place myself in its path. I would almost rather be in the shadow of some object since the sun forces one to write about it).

This is not at all the sort of day to write about Eustache and his dark Parisian world.

***

There is a question to which I return continually (what else do I do but return continually to questions?) although I do not usually allow it to appear for the eyes of others.

***

La Maman was playing the other night and a friend, who had seen me writing in the first notebook, the one with the name "Jean Eustache" on the cover, and had asked about it and been told what I was doing ("writing about the filmmaker Jean Eustache who just killed himself"), had told me and I had said that I didn't want to see it. Why? (It's me asking that question, not my friend.) Not because I have already seen it five or six times but rather because it would be disruptive if, while in the midst of writing this, the film and its relation to my image of it would suddenly intrude in a new form. I don't think I want to see it again for many years, if ever.

***

Is there love, anywhere, in *La Maman*? Just now it seems to me not. There is the desire for it, the need for it, but not the thing itself. I wonder if this is a choice made by the characters or is it merely (wrong word) the result of their disposition to neither give nor receive love?

While making these notes over the last week I have constantly been saying to myself how much I admire the character of Alexandre, how I find nothing in him of which to disapprove, but now I am not so sure. This demonstrates, I suppose, my firm belief that as soon as we say something, it ceases to be true. But this is not the only reason I am changing my mind. Love, or a reasonable facsimile, has appeared. I don't know for how long, or how deep, but whatever it is is making me think in different ways. I'd better stop now, my hands shaking from too many cigarettes, too much coffee and something else?

***

Let me pose a direct question. Does Eustache's suicide make sense? I don't mean only "can one understand why he killed himself?" but also "did the nature of his artistic vision lead in this direction?" I ask this because I see that I am looking at his work differently now.

***

The advantage, or disadvantage, of writing in this notebook everyday, whether I feel like it or not, whether I have something to say about Eustache or not, is that I have a sense of grappling with the physical act of writing.

***

I think that this has been and still is a waiting. I have written nothing about Eustache or at least nothing about him that has been anything like what I wanted to write about him. This inability has partly to do with the loss of those first pages I wrote when still feeling the immediate news of his death. In those pages, which were concise and inspired, I may have said all that I had to say, whatever it was.

***

The presence, significance and pleasure of everyday objects — Eustache makes great use of them in *La Maman.* A door soiled by decades of hands opening and closing it, a bottle of whiskey, a glass, a wash basin, a scarf, a wheel chair. And not just the objects but the way in which they are used. I think one reason the film impressed me so much the first time I saw it was because of the attention it lavished on the actors performing the simplest actions, the way whiskey was poured into a glass, the way someone smoked a cigarette or relished certain phrases. The moment when the actors ceased to act.

***

Last night I told J., who is French, that she reminded me of Bernadette Lafont in *La Maman.* Actually I addressed the observation to her friend who sat across the table in the kitchen of a friend's house. Her friend disagreed with me, but she is also the one who found Eustache's characters such tedious people.

At three o'clock in the morning, after running around town with various people, I telephoned T., who I knew would be sleeping and had to get up early the next morning. The last time we'd spoken she had said that we should see less of each other, because she wanted "to see a lot of different people." Nonetheless, I called her, woke her up and said that I was coming over unless she said no. She didn't. I took a taxi to her place, woke her up again and made love to her in an aggressive manner.

At some point last night in my somewhat intoxicated mind, one of the thoughts that contributed to me deciding that I would in fact break a rule and call T. in the middle of the night and impose myself on her, whether for sex or talk, was that it was something the characters in Eustache's film wouldn't hesitate to do.

***

Much to my surprise, the habit of going from café to café between the hours of twelve and eight each day is beginning to bore me. Luckily, this fatigue coincides with the last pages of the second notebook. These two things — my boredom with café life and the end of the notebook — seem to indicate that I will not write much more about Eustache and his film.

Yesterday I read through what I've written and found, unexpectedly, a few ideas worth developing. Unfortunately I know I'm not going to get around to doing so. Which means, I guess, that I have failed. I don't deny that with respect to any sort of adequate treatment of what ostensibly was my subject, I have failed. But what do I mean by "adequate?" I suppose it means the fulfilling of whatever expectations are raised at the outset, like the adequate lover. But to simply fulfill expectations and nothing more doesn't seem very interesting. Better a mixture of teasing and excess, a pleasurable meandering which allows for those quite natural moments when inspiration is absent, when concentration breaks, when nothing happens. What is important is not knowing what is going to happen next. When I am reading a sentence or paragraph and feel that I know what is going to be said, my mind drifts off.

But that doesn't change my failure. Yet, it seems to me that if you are reading these words, after having read the ones which preceded them, I cannot consider that I have failed, even though I never quite got around to writing what I had wanted to write in the way I wanted to write it. This (what I have written) is instead of that (what I had hoped to write) but since that was impossible, this is instead of nothing.

AUGUST IN OLARA

Above all, no invention. (Nothing is more tedious than a "gifted imagination" at work.) Next, and perhaps last: the pursuit of clarity. But clarity must always be clarity about something; like consciousness, which from time to time it resembles, clarity must have an object in order to exist. The object here is some quotidian events on one of the Balearic Islands. The subject is . . .

If I were still of a rebellious frame of mind, I might say that I have turned to the following material because I just happened to read a few pages of Elio Vittorini's *Conversation In Sicily* or because it is a dreary rainy day in this northern city or because I have to write about something and these notes from last summer will serve as well as the next thing. All of this is true, and yet destiny may still have a role to play; the melting down and recasting of my time in Olara may turn out to have been necessary.

Now you must picture me seated at a green metal table in a small whitewashed room. Old wooden beams run across the sloping ceiling and there is a window in the middle of one wall. The window is small and closed off by roughly made wooden shutters. Between the slats of the shutters you can see parts of some trees and the curved-tile roofs of closely clustered buildings. The sunlight outside the window is very strong and though the room itself is dark, except for the lamp on the metal table, it is breathlessly hot.

On the floor near my feet is a small electric fan whirring back and forth. I am typing (on a small manual Hermes), trying to set down everything I have learned about Olara in the three weeks I've been there. I've started with the neighbors who live just across the narrow stone stairs: Paco, his wife, daughter and an old man who is the father of either Paco or his wife. Close to 80, perhaps even past 80, this old man still walks everyday to their farm house a mile outside of town. Paco is not a farmer — he works in one of the small shoe factories that have been the town's chief source of income for several decades, though the industry is now threatened by foreign competition, chiefly in Asia. The farm house on the two-or-so acres Paco's family owns is a small, two-story stone structure surrounded by a grove of almond trees. The electricity for the light and refrigerator come from a car battery and the water from a well just outside the front door. As far as I have been able to discover there is no plumbing of any kind on the house. Next week David and I will go out and spend a day helping to harvest the almonds.

On the other side of David and Elizabeth's house, across a dead-end alley just large enough for a car to drive through, live Jorge, his wife Ana, and a daughter also named Ana. At present Jorge works as a day laborer building walls along the road outside of town. Ana (the daughter) works in a supermarket in the city and is engaged to Carlos, who is one of the local policemen.

Policemen — there are four of them: two younger ones and two older ones. When I first visited Olara, five years ago, there were only the two older ones, but a year ago they hired Carlos and Lluch, both in their mid-20s. They were not hired because the community had need of two more cops but only to ensure continuity. Each generation requires at least two policemen, so Carlos and Lluch must be in place before the older ones retire. The job is an easy one. There is no crime to speak of and most of their work revolves around automotive problems: blocking off the plaza every Friday for the market, adjudicating parking disputes (when Señor X parks in front of Señor Y's garage) and arriving at the scene of accidents. Of the four policemen, Carlos is by far the nicest, in fact he is one of David and Elizabeth's closest friends.

Between Jorge and Paco, in the corner where the alley and the stairs meet, live a menage à trois (a woman and two men). The story runs: the wife was having an affair for many years but the husband never knew. One day he was in a café when a friend, no longer able to stand by and see his buddy duped, said: "Your wife is having an affair with Z." The husband laughed, it was impossible. The friend replied: "I swear to you that if you go back to your house right now you will find your wife in bed with Z." Still skeptical, the husband returned home and, sure enough, found his wife in bed with Z. Since that day, the story runs, the three of them have lived together in that corner house. They're now in their late 50s.

An unmarried man of around 60 whose name I don't know lives in the house next to Paco. People talk about how primitive his house is: floors of packed dirt, little light and less furniture. The man is friendly in a distant way, never coming over to chat as do Paco, Jorge and their respective households.

Next to the dirt-floor house is one bought a few years ago by a Norwegian artist who only visits Olara twice a year. Last summer she lent David and Elizabeth a large house in the Norwegian countryside, with the stipulation that they not have visitors. Her ostensible reason for this was that she wanted to make sure David wasn't disturbed in his writing, but I suspect that she was also motivated by a Scandinavian fear of disorder. (I also took it personally, even though I had no wish to visit Norway.) I'm dubious about her claims to be an artist — rather she seems to me the wife of a successful man, the mother of two pampered blond beasts and a woman with time on her hands and unfulfilled ambitions towards self-expression which result in watercolors of trees and knitted wall hangings.

The last neighbor I'll mention is a woman who lives down the hill with her large family. She screams at them all day and we call her "the fishwife."

Last night the weather changed from summer to autumn. Strong winds swept away the heat and haze, leaving a comfortable temperature and a sky that seemed to contain every star. When we got home from watching television at Ca'n Roig — Miguel and Silvia's summer home — David and I sat on the terrace looking at the sky, passing a pair of binoculars back and forth. We saw several shooting stars and traded bits of elementary astronomy. This morning it is still cool, but it can't last: we're still in August, in Olara.

The movie we saw last night was one of the "Thin Man" series with William Powell and Myrna Loy. Not a particularly good one but at least it was broadcast in English, with Spanish subtitles. There were a few amusing moments though not even Powell's infallible charm could rescue the film from its dreadful plot and worse characterizations, some of which I found embarrassing. One of the numerous villains was a Cuban who frequented a nightclub — the movie was set in New York City — called "The West Indies." About halfway through the movie there is a musical sequence at this club, complete with "Cuban" dancers — in fact American Blacks. There are, however, some "authentically" Hispanic characters, but without exception they are portrayed in a ridiculous manner. The women chatter endlessly and grab for cigarettes, the men attempt seductions while dancing tangos and whip out enormous knives at the drop of a hat. The accents, clothes, haircuts and social code of these characters set them apart from the perfect deportment of the central white characters. Even the lower class characters — comic white villains — are taken more seriously than the Cubans, making it pretty clear that Americans of 1939 regarded a Spanish accent as a sign of faulty civilization, hence laughable. I worried that Miguel and Silvia would take personally the movie's inane ethnocentrism and suspect that we too harbored such attitudes, but of course they probably didn't identify at all with the pseudo-Cubans.

Yesterday David, Carlos and I went for a bike ride to Lloseta and back — about 15 kilometers. With Carlos setting the pace, we cut 15 minutes off our previous time. The other night, a Sunday, we were about to sit down to dinner on the terrace when Carlos and Ana came by. Carlos always whistles to let us know that he is coming, but that is as much warning as we ever get.

In Olara, no one ever phones — they just come over. David sometimes makes what he calls "preemptive visits." If he gets the feeling that someone may be about to pay him an impromptu visit, he goes to see them, knowing that a 10-minute visit from him will put off a much longer ordeal from them. In any case, we talked with Carlos and Ana for a few minutes and then, when it was clear that they intended to stay, we invited them to join us for dinner. Luckily, there was plenty of food, though only Carlos ate. Halfway through the meal, Ana's father Jorge came over, slightly drunk. He joined us at the table, not seeming to notice his daughter's disapproving looks and Carlos's mocking laughter. Five minutes later his wife came by and what was going to be a quiet dinner for three had become a party of seven. We had a good time, just the same. At one point Elizabeth was asking Ana's mother where she could buy salt cod, explaining that I wanted to make a *brandade*, a French dish I'd just discovered.

Hearing this, Jorge turned to me and said, "Do you cook?"

"A little," I replied.

He said, "Good, then you can come over tomorrow and cook lunch for us."

I responded, jokingly, that I didn't work on Mondays.

"Then you'll come Tuesday."

"How much do you pay," I kidded him.

"In Spain we don't have to pay," he crowed and gave a mock fascist salute and shouted "Francisco Franco!"

Eventually they all drifted back home, but not before Ana brought over some ice cream she had made.

During the fiestas this year there was an exhibition of photographs in the town hall documenting the history of Olara. While David was at the exhibition, an old man came up to him and pointed to a photograph of a man. In 1936, roughly the era of the photo, the man had been the mayor and, at the outbreak of the Civil War, had been shot along with 14 other men from Olara. Then the old man led David to another photograph, a group shot dating from the same period. Pointing to one of the group, he said in a lowered voice, "That's him, that's the leader." (Meaning the leader of the local fascists who had murdered the 14 men.) David asked if he was still alive, and still in Olara. "Yes," the old man whispered.

When David told me this story, I wondered how the community was able to live with such memories. I thought of the children of the murdered men. What was it like to have to pass your father's murderer in the street?

Outside the church, a nondescript early 18th-century building on the plaza, they have recently installed a new memorial to the Civil War dead. While the old memorial only mentioned the Nationalist dead, the new one (a modern sculpture atop a large rock which is set in a long reflecting pool) remembers those who died on both sides. Similar revisionist monuments have been erected throughout Spain in recent years, and no doubt in many towns elderly unpunished murderers walk among the children of their victims.

There are five bars:

Sa Maquina
Bar Tango
Bar Biambo
Traffic
Bar Ibiza

During my last visit, we went mostly to the Tango and the Biambo, sometimes ending up, when it was very late and we were very drunk, at the Maquina — hangout of local misfits. Now the Tango and the Biambo have fallen from grace and everyone goes to Traffic (pronounced *trafeek*). There are also five cafés: Ca'n Tiu, Casino, two whose names I don't know and one we call "the old people's café." There are only two restaurants, the Bar Ibiza (terrible service, medium food — we never go there except during fiestas) and the Meson Gallega, formerly Cama Secas. When it was Cama Secas the only thing on the menu (actually they had no menu) was roast chicken, fried innards and a thick soup. The Meson Gallega opened about two years ago and serves food from the northwestern province of Galicia. It's quite good and they also have vino ribero, a "green" wine I love.

Sometimes, when the wind is blowing in from the east, you can smell the stench of sulfur as you drive into town and, once in a while, there are muffled booms at night, but otherwise you wouldn't know the mines existed. One evening, soon after I arrived, Jorge came by as we were finishing dinner on the terrace. Somehow the mines came up and he began telling us about when he had worked in them. It had been hard and dangerous and badly paid but he was desperate at the time. One detail of his long account particularly struck me: how each crew had someone to watch the roof of the mine tunnel for signs of imminent cave-ins. This person was called a *vigilante*. Survival, Jorge explained, came down to whether you had a good *vigilante* or a bad one. This he called "*la suerte de vigilante*."

Over their years in Olara, David and Elizabeth have invented their own names for the various stores:

the Everything Store
the Bridge Store
the Cross-Eyed Lady's Bakery
the Supermarket Store

Each name describes some salient feature of the store in question and even in the cases where they now know the real names, they continue to use the ones they invented.

Mecky, mecky, mecky, méc; mecky, mecky, mecky, mú.
Muy bien, muy bien, muy bien, muy BIEEEEN.
Viente y dos, viente y dos, viente y dos, viente dos; viente y dos, viente y dos, viente y dos, viente y dos.

These three phrases, incantations of sorts, are said whenever possible by our Olarian friends. They are uttered rapidly and loudly. I don't know their origin, though I think they probably come from television shows and pop songs. There is another one — "gorda, gorda, gorda, super gorda, gorda, gorda" — from a song by the popular group Orchestra Mondragon, which even David comes out with from time to time.

It is another day in Olara. I am again working on the Hermes "Baby" and the room is the same except for an open suitcase lying on the bed. I begin by observing that apparently a week has gone by without me adding to these pages and now I find I am leaving tomorrow with so much still unnoted. I had planned to write at least 500 words a day but the week was too full.

Yesterday, a Monday, David and I went into Amalpa in the morning to go to the bank. Later I bought presents for various people and some books for myself. When we got back at 2, some seafaring Danish friends were here for lunch, which lasted until 7:30. At least that's how long they stayed, playing quinzet and drinking brandy. After they left I rode to Lloseta, arriving home in time for a quick shower and a bowl of cold beans before having to run down to Traffic to meet Hermoine and Roque. (She's English and he's Colombian; they're both stuck in Olara because they don't have enough money or qualifications to start a life elsewhere.) I talked with them until 11:30, drinking four *cañas* (draft beers) and trying to avoid the subject of Elizabeth's obvious animosity toward Hermoine.

The day earlier, Sunday, I woke at noon, with a medium hangover, and in less that an hour found myself in a car with David, Elizabeth, Carlos and Ana on the way up to the mountains for a picnic. There were about twelve of us, from ages 5 to 65, and we had rabbit and sausage grilled over an open fire, *trumpo* (a kind of salad), wine and cognac. After the meal we sang Beatles songs, with me on guitar, and played quinzet. Later Ana's mother danced to traditional local music on a tape given to me at the end of the day by Carlos's father. We stayed there, in a little grove of trees off the side of the road, until about seven. When we came home I tried cooking my *brandade* which came out too salty to eat.

The day before that, Saturday, began at 6:30 AM, as David and I got up and rode our bicycles out to the *campo* to help Paco harvest his almonds. We worked until one, with Paco's wife and daughter helping while the grandfather and an old woman whose status I didn't catch, started shelling the almonds we harvested. Then we started our four hour lunch with Paco and his wife plying us with food and drink until the long morning's work grew distant, as did everything in the world except that small dark room and the weathered, friendly faces around the makeshift, bountiful table.

Finally about five, David and I swooped home on our bikes, arriving in time to start preparing for my *despedida* or going-away party. The guests were: Silvia, Miguel, Carlos, Ana, Jorge and Ana senior. Silvia and Elizabeth made a huge paella and we all sat around the table for a long time. Two marathon meals in one day! At some point we moved to the living room, pushed away all the furniture and started dancing. Since it was my party, I insisted on choosing the records. First loud pop music, to which even Ana senior danced, then a long Pharaoh Sanders number that everyone not only danced to but sang along with, even the normally reserved Miguel. By four in the morning only David, Ana and I remained. Ana and I were seated on the couch, flirting intensely. David was in a chair a few feet away. An early Miles Davis record was playing. Finally, David went up to bed — because, as he told me the next day, he felt like a chaperone — and Ana and I remained on the couch for another half hour, only talking now, rather than tickling each other and finding excuses to join hands and look in each others eyes. It was not that we had been performing for David, rather that his presence allowed us to reveal something like desire by ensuring that it wouldn't develop into anything more. Once he had gone, we had to stop. Why? Because of Carlos, Ana's fiance who at that moment was somewhere making his night rounds. So we spoke, softly almost, gravely, until 4:30 when I sent her home and made my way to a much needed sleep.

How clear one can be! At least on the page. Just saying what happened, or didn't, in the most untreacherous language. Wonderful to be clear, even if it (what actually happened, or didn't) wasn't — except that this clearness wasn't what I mean by clarity. Maybe the kind of clarity I meant isn't possible when one is just saying what happened. Maybe clearness and clarity cancel each other out, like a clean window and a clear sky or two clean windows placed on after the other. No, if this isn't the kind of clarity I meant, it is because by saying what happened, I know what I'm going to say before I say it. It's too easy. Clarity, I'm almost certain, doesn't mean telling old stories (even if they're only a day or a few hours old). But rehearsed clarity is better than none.

Now, having left the island and its ocean, the town and its people, all my old and new friends, five days ago, I find it difficult to return to this text. I am no longer in that dark, hot room. I can't get up and look out the little window at the church, the *ayuntamiento*, the hill with its Virgilian farm. The windows here are many and large and they look out on solidly built, three and four-story, 19th-century houses. I'm staying in a neighborhood which was once home to Engels and Sylvia Plath and it's starting to seem like I was never in Olara at all. I'll only be here a week.

Some store names I forgot to include: the Butter Store, the New Store, the Swiss Air Store (because a guy who works there also has a job at the Amalpa airport with Swiss Air).

David and I had three basic bicycle rides. The shortest, about four kilometers, was to take the road out past the *matador* (the slaughterhouse), turn right along a tree-covered lane that passed a big finca, turn right again and continue until we met the main road into town.

This route had the advantage of being both flat and picturesque, but it was too short to be satisfying. The second ride followed the main road out of town, past the mines, then turning right onto a narrow road that led through olive groves and past a pig farm. Sometimes we'd stop to look at the massive beasts. Continuing, we'd eventually turn right to head back towards town on a small road that climbed up to a hilltop from which you had a nice view of the town. From the top of this hill we'd speed back into Olara from the west.

Our favorite ride began like the first on the road heading east, past the *matador*, but instead of turning off toward the tree-covered lane we continued straight, over a long series of hills which gradually, exhaustingly, led to the top of a small mountain. The road down from there was the route's chief attraction: a 10-minute, high-speed coast where the only thing you needed were good brakes for the more dangerous curves. By the time we reached the bottom, after which we tried to keep moving for as long as possible without pedaling, we were a good distance away from Olara. Turning south, we met a new road which we turned onto, heading west. It was smooth and fast and led us past olive trees, a quarry, a small town with a very Arabic-sounding name which was noted (at least in the immediate area) for its wine, a windmill and several aggressive dogs — easily outrun. This road eventually brought us onto the main Olara road but much further away that the first ride, which meant that we had a steady uphill ride for the last 15 minutes. No matter how hot it was or how much I'd drunk the night before, I tried to take one of these rides (usually the third, longest one) every day. Once in a while, Carlos would join us but he tended to set a faster pace than we liked, turning it into a race.

Eventually, if you've known them a while, older people in Olara will describe the years after the Civil War to you. "There was nothing to eat." they'll say. "We were always hungry."

I haven't said anything about what everyone looks like or how I feel about them. I've left out most of the other foreigners and Pep and Carmen, and Toni of the Ca'n Tiu, and the fiestas.

At least I'll get in the *traca final*. On the last day of the fiestas, sometime after midnight, everyone drifts into the plaza. They mill around, drinking beer, feeling both relieved and let down that the wild week is coming to an end, that summer is drawing to a close.

Trees surround the plaza and on a nail driven into each tree, the *traca* — a several-hundred-foot-long cord laced with a multitude of powerful firecrackers — is strung. Suddenly someone lights it and for a long minute the plaza is filled with hundreds of booms and flashes as the fuse sputters from tree to tree. Even though you are ready for the *traca*, you can't help but flinch once or twice when a really big one goes off too close. When it's over, everyone applauds and then slips away from the smoke-filled center of town, purged of whatever sins they may have committed during the fiestas, making their way through the shadowy, narrow streets back toward the rest of life.

MR. INFO.

(for Noël Dolla)

It was the period between the auto-demolition of the People's Democracies and the referenda on Maastricht; Yves Montand, Klaus Barbie and Doctor Seuss had all recently passed over; numerous heads of state confessed to the authorship of pseudonymously published short stories and poems on ecological themes; average prices of works of art began to fall dramatically, although most other commodities remained stable; it was the time of the completion of several vast construction projects, among them a dam, a tunnel . . .

I had decided that year to sublet my place in literature to another, in order to turn my attention to what seemed of more pressing interest. Having recently completed a certain project there seemed no point in continuing along such a route, at least for the moment. I wasn't certain that I was prepared for my new activity, having never had the vigorous training which I assumed was required for such investigations, but . . .

After an absence of some years, the new was returning. All at once, individual after individual began to think of their lives as . . .

He was still hoping, any day now, to catch up with the articles (book reviews, editorial columns, scientific breakthroughs) from two and a half years ago. He was always at a table in the back of the café, slowly reading a carefully cut out piece of newsprint or paging through his agenda, checking dates and addresses. We called him "Mr. Info."

It was in the period around the fall of Gorbachev, a little before or after doesn't matter. Suffice to say that there was uncertainty in the air, that Dr. Seuss and Klaus Barbie were both dead, that many had given up waiting for signs of a new spirit and were content to plod on with their given talents, recalling the image of the gaunt scholar with the bitter laurels, wrapped in a shroud of night and serenity.

I, for my sins, was sitting by a window of the Milano-Marseille express reading the *TLS*. Since Genova I'd had the compartment to myself and was as content as anyone in my position could expect to be.

The review of a recent novel by one of my compatriots, satisfyingly negative nonetheless reminded me that I had ceded to others the center. The phrase "I would never . . ." ran through my head, slipping in and out of sync with the wheels of the train. I felt regret but also satisfaction. At the continual risk of utter disappearance, I still had an open road, or several of them. I had not played my hand.

We pulled in to Ventimiglia and I readied myself for Italian and French customs who would shortly be boarding the train.

We let ourselves in for ordeals that seem so pointless and avoidable to others. Only when looking back do we understand why they found our behavior so hard to understand.

There . . . (illegible) . . . few years of . . . (illegible) . . . explain to . . . (illegible) . . . suffered in . . . (illegible) . . . my actions or inactions. I hope they . . . (illegible) . . . not able to just now. Perhaps some other day, when I have more time.

The ones I can never identify in the photo are Baziotes (or Molotov or Sutcliff) and Brooks (or Dulles or Best) but having finally put this limit of my knowledge down in writing I feel that I have magically overcome it, that next time I meet those faces, I'll know them by name.

Customs agent enters compartment and finds only one adult male proffering one U.S. passport. Agent takes said passport and starts to violently turn its pages with an ungainly thumb. "You travel a lot, Mr. (glances back at the passport) Rubbishshelf." (Fixes penetrating gaze on aforementioned adult male, then looks at passport again) "Barcelona, Linate, London, Amsterdam. A lot of traveling. What is it" (a note of distinct menace intrudes) "exactly that you do?"

(pleasantly) "I am an art critic."

Clearly nonplused by this answer but determined not to show it, customs agent puts on a show of sudden or, perhaps, sincere amusement. "Ah, do you know Vittorio Sgarbi?"

American traveler wonders if this is a test or if official really wants to know if he knows aforesaid personage. “I know who he is, of course, but I have not made his acquaintance. He is very well known.”

In translation from mouth of American to brain of customs agent this becomes a claim of close personal friendship with that ubiquitous T.V. personality, Sg. Sgarbi, the man who has given the Italian public an image of the art critic as a publicity-mad womanizer of unrbidled arrogance and political ambition.

The agent, with a large smile, hands back the passport and as he leaves the compartment he shouts to a colleague down the corridor: “Hey Gianni, get this! There’s an American art critic here who’s good pals with Vittorio Sgarbi!”

I read in the paper the other day that the comic-book hero of my childhood had in fact been modeled on a notorious European fascist, an enthusiastic collaborator with the Nazis, who remains to this day in Spain, safe, unextraditable.

Marseilles-Milan Express

Didn’t have time yesterday to make notes. Just remembered hearing L.T. on the BBC World Service a couple of weeks ago, speaking about her latest novel, just published in the U.K. She talked about how much information is conveyed simply by putting a place-name at the head of a text. I was reminded of Larbaud. This came to mind just now because I debated putting “Nice” at the head of this text. If I had found (or made, if one must be honest) the time yesterday to write, I could have done so, but now since I am no longer in Nice, this page must bear a different heading.

While in Nice I was granted a glance into one of Mr. Info’s notebooks. I found this: “In the middle of page two of today’s *IHT*, a photograph of a group of German neo-Nazis saluting. ‘ON THE MARCH — Neo-Nazis giving a fascist salute during a weekend demonstration in Bonn denouncing foreigners,’ the caption reads. The central figure is an overweight fellow who looks to be in his early 20s. His right arm is raised in the appropriate fashion. He wears a dark zippered jacket, the left arm of which has a small pocket with a zipper. He is carrying a large drum attached to his body by a thick leather strap across his chest. His left hand holds two drumsticks. His light colored hair is cut short and parted to one side in an obvious attempt at a Hilterian coif. Behind him stands another younger looking adherent, dressed in a similar jacket and wearing a military cap. We can see part of the trumpet or horn he is holding. There are at least another four neo-Nazis visible in the photo, although one gets the impression that they are part of a considerably larger crowd. One on the left carries a drum decorated with a rising-flame motif, which is also visible on the other drum. Another holds a horn of some sort. Two are skinheads. Drummer #2 has a hood pulled up over his head. One of the skinheads has a bandana covering his nose and mouth. The mouths of the first two figures are open. They could be singing."

Late at night in a hotel room: E is asleep and I'm watching a documentary on Rossellini. The sound is turned down low but I can still hear the screenwriter of *Rome: Open City* account for the movie's style and power: "We had just come out of a dictatorship and we were glad to be able to tell the truth — that's the secret."

Here is the plan which I promised you earlier. I guess I will have to trust you not to reveal it to any of our competitors. And if you want to put it into operation yourself, why should that bother me? [Once someone took a cadence from me who shouldn't have; his parents visit his grave every Sunday.] Anyway, it went like this: I made a list of 12 writers, some of them friends, some figures I admired. To each I sent a list of characters, along with some specifications as to time of year and day, locale, etc. I then asked each one to write a very brief synopsis of one chapter of a novel using the information I had supplied and mail it back to me. These twelve synopses formed a set of instructions for my latest novel. What I did was simply write a dozen chapters according to the ideas they furnished. [All royalties will be divided accordingly.]

"The general theme of the Congress will be Aesthetics, Daily Life and the Arts. There will be six sections: 1. Rules of the Game. 2. The Last Days. 3. The Voice of Things. 4. How to Imagine. 5. The Regrets. 6. In The Future Perfect. Members wishing to participate should communicate with: German Organizing Committee, c/o Prof. Urs Graf,

Niebuhrstrasse 19, 53 Bonn, W. Germany. Papers — on no account exceeding 100,000 words — should be sent to this address not later than 1st February."

To be submitted for further study: "Too few of you, too many of me."

21% have never heard it mentioned
2% have a very positive opinion of it
3% have a fairly positive opinion
5% think they won the war
3% think they came to power in the 1950s

It was in the run-up to the regional elections and many of us expected the worst and were a little disappointed with the inconclusive results. It meant that they were still able to work in darkness, spreading silently, saliently.

Then later there were the farmer protests, the trucker protests, the mechanic protests, the bank clerks' strike, the screenwriters' walkout. Things were getting so bad that there were not only counter protests but also counter strikes. When the writers' strike came, the printers walked out of their jobs not in sympathy but to show their anger at the writers for striking and thus robbing them, the printers, of their livelihood.

It seems so simple "on paper" as they say — here the expression is inappropriate — but the form is elusive. Only recently am I learning to be content with the gap, and thus notice its incremental shrinkage.

I'm not completely at ease about my name sitting there to the right of the door for all to see. That doesn't mean I think it's all going to end badly again, and yet . . .

What this has to do with that, I don't know, except that it was more or less the same place where all these things happened.

A promise is a reference to another statement, a statement-to-come.

If we now review our arguments — 1. the perilous path, 2. the bleached bones, 3. the just man, 4. the hungry clouds — we have a considerable number of clues at our disposal suggesting how it came about that these events passed so utterly unremarked.

Wandering around near the old port, I ran into an acquaintance of Mr. Info's. He was a painter, with a peculiar method of working. A right-handed man, he painted only with his left hand (tying the right one behind his back). Furthermore, while painting he always wore a patch over one, perfectly good eye, leaving the other to struggle on by itself. His subjects were inevitably portraits, rough-looking heads, of what he liked to call the "citizens of the Côte de Chernobyl."

We stopped in to the Café de Turin for a carafe of wine and a few oysters. I inquired after our mutual friend. The painter fished a postcard out of his coat pocket and handed it to me. The card was of the cheapest kind, blank on both sides. Its only advantage, that of having more space for the text, the sender ignored, writing in blue ball-point only two lines:

> It takes a long time to hear
> the voice of your own wound.

POSTE RESTANTE

(in memory of Georges Guy)

They have retreated back into their discrete categories and no longer compete for our attention. The debate has been suspended, the symposium called off. But on a table, in a small whitewashed building near the sedate harbor, a chance arrangement of objects leads to a few hours of leisurely cartography, to the adjournment of adjournment. On one side of the typewriter (otherwise known as literature) is the ashtray (otherwise known as philosophy), and on the other side is the cooling cup of coffee (otherwise known as science). Between them a letter is being written.

Dear D.,

I posit a question in a distant discipline, somewhere beyond the horizon of my abilities and inclinations, then allow it to come towards me in a series of leaps, rushing over the landscape of discourse as if by heliography. Call it: a light endowed with memory whose path is charted by means of black lines. Call it: graphic deduction.

Must the search for truth succeed?

For years I repeated to myself, and still do, despite the skepticism which has accrued with my consciousness of that repetition, that only after a certain degree of attainment would I become capable of joining the others.

My mistake up until this moment has been the assumption that such an attainment would involve a pause, that it would take the form of a crest or pinnacle, a border crossing, an abyss. Why not, instead, a billboard on the side of the road I failed to notice because of that curious formation of clouds off to the left, or an obscure station passed in the middle of the night by a curtained express?

No answer, while the murmur of postponement continues.

Suddenly, if one can call sudden a divorce which has been in rehearsal for years, each break, each reconcilement, more vivid, more violent than the last, suddenly I am "unable to write." By this I mean that none of the convenient ports have names for me. Lying offshore at tentative anchor, I pace the deck, cursing the numbered berths I cannot approach.

I have spent most of today, Sunday, reading S. I read his long essay on M.P. and the first chapter of *What Is Litmus?* Why? Who reads S. these days?

Lately I have been disinclined to be taken out of myself and being unable to write has only exacerbated this condition. I no longer go to movies, with the exception of an occasional documentary, and to attempt reading a novel requires huge amounts of enthusiasm and free time. Any cultural activity — museums, galleries, concerts, restaurants (in this city, at this time, restaurants are a cultural activity, perhaps the chief one) — seems less preferable than walking a quiet street, having a drink in a nondescript bar, washing dishes while listening to the radio, spending a day reading J.P.S.

Finished, if only temporarily, with literature, I turn to the genre that still seems to me the most natural version of ourselves available to us.

Philosophy, a poetic biography of not so much its author as its reader . . .

ANOTHER LETTER

Dear T.,

Just now the various projects awaiting my hand, and even the siren-filled void where you go to meet the new work, seem not worth turning to — I feel that I already know the face of anything I might write too well and the phrases that would issue from its mouth are as predictable as the bad news at the end of Greek myths.

For proportion, wisdom and efficiency, there is nothing I admire more than those few pages G.G. published in September 1952, some three years before you and I were given our bodies and names. How did it begin? "Remember, Théo: truth won at last or subjectivity appropriated by us . . . the strangeness of our roads. We had to appear . . . ."

Do you remember that day in 1979 when we kept at assignation made many months before, on another continent? The Café F. was closed and you were waiting in front of the Brasserie L. across the street.

Last night I dreamt about Nancy P. Not the Nancy P. from Malibu but the other one. In my dream she was just as I remember her being then . . .

RETURN TO THE FIRST LETTER

. . . That indispensable role filled by the reader's agreement, a contract of syntax.

"All literature which refuses to march fraternally between science and philosophy is a homicidal and suicidal literature."

This from the man (C.B.) who had such doubts about Progress! In fact, such a literature did not appear until P.V.

V's achievement was based on the exclusion of dramatic means from literature. Like his creation M.T., he had "killed the marionette." This did not require an extinction of the author's personality in the work — far from it — but an intention to treat the I, the Me, as an object among others. The tastes, inclinations and moods of P.V. were neither the source nor the rasion d'être of his writing, they were instead the only possible material from which that writing could be drawn.

No, that's not quite it. Two points: 1. The realm to which V. restricted himself was his thought, his mind at work, the life of the intelligence . . .

A THIRD LETTER

Dearest E.,

It's Sunday night. I arrived here Thursday afternoon and this is my first chance to write to you. In one way it was very easy to return here, but it's also very difficult. I return to find the accouterments of a life which was mine a year ago but which has now become the life of another, or of no one. My past is dead, as maybe pasts always must be, and I must begin building what that Italian poet called a "new life."

A FOURTH LETTER

Dear M.R.,

Remind me one day to ask your mother if it was near her home in the village of C. that the poet W.W. came across those "black, dripping crags" which C.S. once enthused over to me, remembering how her (and my) poetry teacher A.F. had once emphasized them. And T.B., I think, also once cited the passage to me, particularly the point where the shepherd informs W.W. that he has indeed crossed the Alps. Was T.B. also a student of A.F. or did his interest in the passage have something to do with his frequent visits to your mother?

THE SECOND LETTER, AGAIN

As I look over the top of the typewriter I see the small, brightly lit entryway and the black overcoat and blue umbrella hanging there. They were both here when I arrived, forgotten or abandoned by the previous tenant. Their message is that it can be rainy and cold in this city. Actually, I've already had to use the umbrella a couple of times. (The coat doesn't fit me.) To the right of the entryway, across the room from where I'm sitting, is a bulbous, dark green sofa, long enough for four people to sit on or for one to sleep.

To tenaciously render the terror delicious. What terror? No, it would be more accurate, and less histrionic, to snip off the first letter and say instead: to tenaciously render the error delicious, leaving the t of tenaciously to help suggest only the slightest flavor of terror.

FROM A LETTER WITH NO NUMBER

Odd things come back to me, like the day I noticed the following three details on my way to the Via Ariosto: 1. a man in the flower stand near the Cimitero Monumentale, his round glasses looming out from the dark interior of the stand like white flowers. 2. two policemen on horseback, smiling at the world as if they were out for a leisurely ride. 3. a woman on top of a ladder on the sidewalk washing her shop window, her shoes left neatly at the bottom of the ladder where she'd slipped out of them to climb.

THE FIRST LETTER, RETURNED TO

2. His written relationship to that realm: an assumption that examination of it was sufficient. He said about the philosopher R.D.: "It occurred to him to claim that there is no richer poetic material in the world . . . that the life of the intelligence constitutes an incomparable lyric universe." But he also said: "Having observed that philosophy, psychology and history were useless in the problems that thrust themselves upon me personally, that were born of me, I have considered them as alien — and their values as conventional. Moreover, their characteristic problems seemed rather arbitrary to me. Their difficulties were not mine; I would never have invented them. And to me, their solutions were without force."

ANOTHER LOOK AT THE THIRD LETTER

Today a letter of yours came. I hope you won't mind if I translate some of it into English: "Since you left I've begun to think a lot. I think that we live in a very difficult moment. It seems to me that I can't find anything to which I can attach myself. It seems to me that everything that was certain is in the process of destroying itself. The past is in the process of destroying itself . . . (here follows an account of your dealer visiting your studio) . . . but when he left I felt I was the only one in the world to believe in an idea. I thought a lot. But if I feel that I'm unique in the world, ah well, that's to say that I feel I'm the only one in the world to work. For me that's what work is. It's to believe in an idea . . . I believe that the heart of artists is like a thermometer. Now I would like to measure it."

It's late now. I should go to sleep, to dream that greatest of dreams: that we are together.

I'll write again very soon.

FIRST LETTER, LAST TIME

Today I found in S. some rather nasty comments on V. I can't judge. Maybe V. did "frequent princes, queens, powerful industrialists, dining at their tables . . . working for them." But people have said much worse about S. My love for their books makes allowances, it understands even when it can't understand.

The question of exercise, of transforming this gaze upon a distant constellation into an act of navigation cannot be suspended much longer. It will soon be dawn in the harbor. *The Transgression of the Egress* and *Mont-de-pietie Tête-à-queue* will be replaced on the shelf, not too far apart. The light will go off in the little room and we will walk down to the pier where one communicating vessel or another is waiting for an invitation to a voyage from some eloquent wind.

A GODARD SCRAPBOOK

I am playing with the idea of keeping to a strictly chronological structure, starting with the first word and finishing with the last. (Not so obvious as it sounds.) But I haven't decided about that (or a lot of other things) yet. I need some time, considering that 10 minutes ago I wasn't even sure if this was going to be about Jean Eustache or Jean-Luc Godard. But before I wrote the first word I did decide — this is about Jean-Luc Godard.

1975. I'm 19, an aspiring poet, living in Oakland, Calif., on a combination of inheritance and social security, both of which I am dimly aware will not last for much longer.

That same year Godard is 45 and collaborating with Anne Marie Mieville on *Numéro Deux*, a work shot on video and transfered to film whose title has at least three references: a) women ("The Second Sex"), b) shitting ("number two") and c) that the budget and producer are identical to Godard's first feature, *Breathless*.

My 22-year-old girlfriend is an art student, an aspiring filmmaker. She takes me to see a number of Godard films at the art school she attends. I think we saw *Weekend* and *La Chinoise*. I may have already seen *Breathless* on my own. After that, very rapidly, I'm not sure where, I see every movie Godard made in the '60s, so that by the time she and I break up, a year later, I am better versed in J.L.G.'s films than in the work of any writer with the possible exception of Hemingway, Fitzgerald and — how could I forget? — Ian Fleming.

What good does this do me? It makes me feel that whatever I might achieve in poetry will be a poor substitute for the exciting possibilities of film. But I don't enroll in film school or move to L.A. In my early 20s, I make a couple of experiments in Super 8 and video before lapsing back into the more accessible medium of my portable Hermes typewriter. Years later this is my solution: writing about Godard (though now I use a Toshiba computer instead of the Hermes.)

1998. I'm 43 and making extensive changes to a manuscript which a publisher has already accepted and which I have even sent out for blurbs. Late, but not too late, I hope, I've realized that many passages need revising and even more need to be cut. I also take out entire sections. At the last minute, however, I put one of these deleted texts back into the manuscript, scattering it throughout "A Godard Scrapbook." It's called:

ONCE UPON A TIME IN THE WEST

A month ago, at a dinner following an opening of a show of Philip Guston's "poem-pictures" (the drawings he did with poets, including Clark Coolidge, who has sprinkled his writings with allusions to J.L.G.), I found myself seated next to a woman who, I discovered (the way dinner companions eventually find the points where their lives and interests cross), had actually met and worked for Eustache. She and I had both been fans of Godard and Eustache, she carrying things to the point of getting a job that took her into their world. Now she does something else. For her, as for me, they (and her passion for them) belong to the past. As we ate and drank at the expense of the posh prep school where the show was, pouring out our long held stock of achingly useless information about French Cinema 1965-75, I wondered what there was to do with such closed chapters. This, I guess, is one answer.

It was the time of the World Trade Center bomb and the kickback scandals in Italy. It was the time of the Bombay bombs and the U.S. airdrops in Bosnia. Clinton had been in office for a few months. George Foreman was attempting a comeback somewhere, the Whitney museum had commissioned an artist to build a life-sized toy fire engine and park it on Madison Avenue for the duration of the 1993 Biennial.

Two weeks later I remembered none of these things.

Where so many other "serious" filmmakers knock themselves out trying to penetrate into the inner lives of their characters, Godard manages, over and over, to penetrate into the inner lives of us, his viewers, by proclaiming his actors' perfect lack of interiority:

In *Les Carabiniers*, two characters hold magazine ads for underwear in front of their bodies.

In *Le Petit Soldat* there's a gunman in a car hiding his face with a copy of *L'Express* showing Hitler on the cover

In *Breathless*, Jean Seberg says: "I'd like to know what's behind your face. I've been watching it for ten minutes and I know nothing, nothing."

In *Two or Three Things*, the commentary (spoken by J.L.G.) explains: "She is Juliette Janson. She lives here. She is wearing a sweater with blue stripes. She's got fair hair, or maybe light brown. I'm not sure."

It is almost time to say: "in any case, what else can I do?" It is almost time for "acceptance," but not yet. What it is time for is to drop all the stratagems of clever reservation by which we withdraw support not through any outright "no vote" but by repeated abstention and half-heartedly stiffled giggles at critical points of major addresses.

Returning to New York after a long stay in a foreign country, I have surrounded myself with magazines of all genres (art, fashion, literary, travel, architecture) in order to reacclimate myself to the excess flow of images and ideas, of people and products, that defines life in this place. At random I find:

"MD: Did you purposely set out to make *Bad Lieutenant* look different from *King of New York*?
AF: You know the economics of a film determines the look of it, determines everything. Like Godard said, 'The economics of a film are the politics of a film.' The difference in the look of the films is the difference between the needs of Harvey Keitel versus the needs of

Christopher Walken.

...

MD: What do you think about violence in movies?
AF: Right now I think it's all pussy, man. But what is violence? In a movie, to keep quoting Godard, 'A gun going off is not a gun going off.' Violence in the movies — it's an attitude, it's aggression. And these films weren't made for kids. You're not going to take a three-year-old to a burlesque." ("Malice towards Nuns: Manohla Dargis talks with Abel Ferrara" *Artforum*, March 1993)

In an article titled "The Return of the Gamine" (*Vogue*, January 1993) there is a still from *Breathless* showing Seberg and Belmondo walking out of a café. It's from the Champs Elysées sequence where she's wearing the *New York Herald Tribune* T-shirt. The author explains: "In the 1950s, Audrey Hepburn, Jean Seberg, and Leslie Caron were in the gamine lineup, but they were a little too early and too edgy for mass imitation."

Now there are two ways of establishing the scene. One is to look through this keyhole. What do you see? A tangle of limbs and sheets in a half-lit room? A man leaning against the wall, smoking while a record plays? Or there is the other way: taking a walk along the street or by the side of the lake, alone or with a companion.

"A word isn't what you think it is, it's what you want it to be," your friend says, as if thinking aloud.

On the subway this afternoon, on my way to Long Island City (where I am organizing "Postcards from Alphaville," an exhibition of art with references to J.L.G.), I conceived a novel structured around various scenes or sequences from different Godard films. The point, the hard work, would be to write a narrative that would link these scenes together. For instance, take the scene from *Breathless* where . . . (a very good idea that I am too harried to deal with now).

The same still from *Breathless* that was in the January *Vogue* has turned up again in the July *Harper's Bazaar.* (I'm reading a lot of fashion magazines just now because, unable to make a living writing for art magazines, I'm thinking of trying to write articles for them.) It's on the upper righthand corner of a page of some 40 tiny photos illustrating an article on the history of the T-shirt. Here's the relevant passage:

"Anyone who saw the real-life Jean Sebergs outside the American Express office in Paris in the late '50s knew that something big and different was happening. And the T-shirt was the marker for the change.

That image was so startling that the others copied it almost immediately. Jean-Luc Godard dressed Jean Seberg (an American in Paris in life as in cinema) in a Trib T-shirt, and the look was etched in the popular historical memory for all time."

BBC, April 1, 1992: "Listen to this song by Talking Heads. Can you be sure it's ironic?" says British leftist neo-folkie punk Billy Bragg, taking aim at his American colleagues as he introduces "Don't Worry About The Government."

I'm a guest at someone's house in the country. I take down a copy of a stuffy American literary journal from 1968 and read the following: "A characteristic sample of what I have in mind is a statement made by the Times (London) film critic in defense of Godard's *Made in U.S.A.*: 'If, instead of trying to decipher its political significance, if any, we said it was a film "about" the relationship between a shot of a cold white wall with "Liberté" scrawled across it in blue and the immediately succeeding shot of Anna Karina against a burning yellow door which fills the entire frame, we should probably be much nearer the mark.' Which mark, Mr. Taylor? (Prithee, let's talk fustian a little and gull them!) If audience sensibilities were not so uncertainly lodged between the barbarian and the chic-at-heart, few films given votes of confidence lately would survive any more serious analysis than the foregoing. The 'advanced cinema' audience has been brainwashed by film journalists who follow the bent of their cousins, the art critics: when the object yields no pleasure, invent some, or resign yourself to having no professional justification."

The author is some idiot named Vernon Young, the article is titled "Poetry, Politics and Pornography" and it appeared in the Winter 1967-68 issue of the *Hudson Review.*

It was the second or third time I'd discovered that moment in '66 and '67 when they seemed to be dissolving in a manner that I find fascinating and pleasurable. What makes this moment of lost direction compelling is that it results from (1) a historical force to which those five men were simultaneously inescapably subject and to a certain extent the initiators of and (2) their ambition outstripping their talent or ability.

Their failure can be contrasted with the success of four other men, their compatriots and contemporaries, who found themselves in a similar position but managed to succeed where these others failed. (The Rolling Stones)

He is Raphael Rubinstein. He is a writer. He is wearing a black and white striped t-shirt, tan pants, black tennis shoes. He is of Russian Jewish, Mexican and Scottish extraction. His hair is dark brown or black (I'm not exactly sure which) with a noticable amount of grey.

We'll save it with the images so don't worry too much about the words — but I can't say that since the book in which this text may one day appear will probably have no images, except, perhaps, a black-and-white photo of the author and, who knows, a still from *Alphaville* on the cover.

October 1, 1992
To: Jean-Luc Godard
Fax: 33 1 47 47 22 62

Cher M. Godard,

Un peintre pop anglais en 1963, un artiste conceptuel Americain en 1968, un photographe Allemand en 1984, et une autre dizaine des jeunes artistes dans les dernier cinq années — tous ont fait oeuvres d'art avec references aux vos films.

J'ai organisé une exposition au Musée P.S. 1 à New York (je suis un critique d'art Americain et parfois j'organise des expositions comme celui-ci) dans laquelle j'ai mis tous les oeuvres que je puisse trouver qui parle de vous et de vos films. Puisque votre oeuvre est si plein des references à la peinture, il me semble juste que la peinture (et sculpture, etc) retourne le compliment.

Je veut vous inviter à voire l'exposition, qui s'appele "Postcards From Alphaville: Jean-Luc Godard in Contemporary Art 1963-1992" et qui inaugura le 8 Novembre, Dimanche, 1992. Il sera possible, si tout va bien, de la voire quelques jours avant.

En tous cas, j'attendre le retropectif a MoMA et j'espere de vous recontrer si vous venez a New York dans ses jours la.

Please forgive my less than perfect French.
Sincerely,

. . . if he were still alive what would he be like? What would we be like? He retreated, known only to those who worked in other materials, who were younger than he was. Then, he emerged with his decade of work which set the stage for what followed in the decade he died on the threshhold of. Now a new decade. In what way is it his? Or: how do we look at him now, when it is not simply or merely as a precursor?

Last week he came up twice. Once an older

critic described how he, the critic, had written the first article devoted to his, the artist's, work in 1955 or was it '56, but the magazine did not publish the article until 1959, because the editor was supporting another painter of a different kind. The second time A. R. and I were in Montclair, New Jersey — where he had a series of paintings hanging in the local museum — and we came upon a small painting from 1979 and talked about it. (Philip Guston)

On page 112, near the end of the little book, that's now lying open, cover up, on my lap as I write these words, there's a photo of J.L.G. (now I'm going to pick up the book so I can see the picture again and once I've looked at it, I'll put it down and start to write again, at least I hope that's the way its going to go) on his knees in a field of grass. What is he doing? (There's a 5-story modern building in the background.) He's arranging a dozen packages for a shot. On page 111 there's a description of the shot. I translate (from French to English) this translation (from film to writing): "A medium close-up of a couple who illustrate an ad for Hollywood chewing gum. Backward zoom to show a group of consumer products arranged to suggest a modern city. In the center the happy couple of the photograph surrounded by boxes of: Lava, Omo, Dash, Ajax, Shick razor blades, Lustucru pasta, various brands of cigarettes."

The voiceover, in his voice, says: "I forgot everything, except that, since I'm going back to zero, that's where you have to begin again."

Let's pretend, for the next several pages, that there is a film and I'm writing the commentary.

First the title: *Commentary for an Unmade Film*.

Then a montage of shots of people in the streets of a city, not immediately recognizable. A voice is saying:

"Assume an image. I have one in my head and, for this game to work, you too, the reader, need to do likewise. The odds are that the images we have each imagined will be as different as night and day but that can't be helped, and for reasons I do not yet understand I cannot simply tell you what the image that I have imagined is.

I can tell you what it is not: it is not the face of a dead actress (here, if this really were a film, would be the visage of Jean Seberg); it is not a snow capped mountain peak (Fuji, Shasta); it is not a Louis XIV chair (a shadowy room in Versailles); it is not a small animal (a kitten lapping from a bowl of milk); and so on.

Now, everything I have said until now, and I have said nothing, has been as if this 'commentary' were only a piece of writing accompanying no sort of film, not even an imaginary one. Perhaps the film hasn't begun yet. Each member of the audience has been supplied with a program, as in the theater. On one page of the program this text will be found. Latecomers are given an extra minute or two to read these lines before the lights dim, as they are now doing. In a matter of seconds your surroundings are reduced to shadows, only to right and left is the red glow of the exit signs. A light swells up behind the curtain which is now drawing open to reveal the shimmering screen. Then, simultaneously, music and image begin, the first image of the film comes to life before you. Then, momentarily, at the appropriate moment a voice starts speaking."

What is happening here, in this imaginary (or unmade) film is that the text for an unmade (or imaginary) film is being used for a real (or made) film. But the images on the screen are not the ones the writer (the frustrated filmmaker) is imagining in his commentary. We are not shown Jean Seberg or Mount Shasta when he says their names. Why is this? Because the two works were made independently of each other and have been put together in this fashion by a third person, someone neither the writer or the film maker. Who is this person? She is a woman. She is Marina.

I just found a photograph of Marina taken in the mid-1950s.

Three months ago, at the Museum of Modern Art, I finally saw J.L.G. in person for the first time. I had hoped to see and even meet him a few years earlier. MOMA was mounting a retrospective of his films and videos and the French embassy had arranged a lunch in his honor to which I was invited. The day before the opening, Godard sent the museum a telegram saying that he was too busy shooting his new film and couldn't come to New York. I was disappointed, of course, but also impressed at how cooly Godard had snubbed the world's most prestigious museum of modern art.

Apparently he has a reputation for this kind of behaviour, and also a disdain for museums. Some told me a story about a curator from the Pompidou Center in Paris calling Godard to include one of his works in an exhibition. "Call me back in 20 years!" Godard responded and hung up.

But eventually, at his convenience, Godard showed up at MOMA with an episode from his series *Histoire(s) du Cinema* and I went to see him. After the film, the first response from the audience came from a woman who asked some stupidly aggressive question about Truffaut. Embarassed for her and for New York cinephiles in general, I made sure, by waving my hand and fixing my eyes on the curator/translator standing at the filmmaker's side, that my question was next.

"Why," I wondered, "are there so many still images in your history of moving pictures?"

In the black-and-white photograph Marina is wearing a light colored, embroidered dress which, in the style of the period, billows out below the waist like a tent. She is standing sideways to the camera. The striking things are her bare arm (in startling contrast to the expanse of cloth used for the dress), the hint of buckteeth in her slightly opened mouth and, in the fuzzy background, a train barrier.

Without the identifying caption in the back of the book ("Marina Vlady. Gottingen 1954, the actress is wearing a Film und Frau model. While filming *Sie* ('She'), Directed by Gabor von Vaszary. (Film und Frau 14/1954 Marina's sixteenth birthday).") I would never have recognized her as the "star" of J.L.G.'s *2 or 3 Things I Know About Her.*

I find — who cares — on page 259 — big shit — a poet quoted — so — as follows: "And Jean-Luc Godard last night on television spoke of his movies as 'The train, not the station, because I am no longer waiting.'"

On the cover of the book, I notice several minutes later, is a photograph taken from inside the building where I did "Postcards From Alphaville."

A couple of years ago in Paris I found a book called *Vous avez dit Godard?* in which a French journalist/novelist recounts his obsession with J.L.G. It's a pathetic effort, with the worst kind of self-consciousness and the most dreary anecdotes, neither sufficiently sincere nor ironic.

At the risk of seeming to protest too much: I am not, despite appearances, obsessed with Godard. His movies, yes.

It was the year the secret cache of Aldo Moro's letters was discovered hidden in the false wall of an apartment where the kidnapped politician had been held prior to his murder. The police had been

in possession of this apartment for over twelve years, yet had never found the letters until now. Perhaps this was some kind of "Purloined Letter" situation where the hiding place had been overlooked because it had been so obvious.

If I write about J.L.G. (his films), it is for some very specific reasons, which maybe I'll set forth in a moment, but I just remembered seeing *Caro Diario* a week ago and how I thought about it being a much more reasonable model for me as a writer. And yet, here I am, a rainy Sunday afternoon, trying for the thousandth time to reconcile my admiration for J.L.G. with my inability to do what he does.

Well, the truth is, if J.L.G.'s work has any valuable influence on my own, it will not be in texts like this one.

Maybe I should have written about Eustache, or Nanni Moretti. In any case, in a few minutes I'll have to turn to something else — time is almost up for "shooting" this Godard "documentary."

Everything is preparation for a moment that, in turn, justifies the preparation. A whole movie is made in order to arrive at the last shot and the last shot has to support all that came before.

All I'm trying to do is reach a moment (that coincides with a page) in which I can put things clearly, in which I can explain to you (and myself) why those certain minutes or seconds of *2 or 3 Things* or *Masculin Feminine* leave me completely full and completely empty, why they occupy my senses, why they make me feel this (or at least something else I'll figure out after the movie is over) is why I am living.

Last week I went to see a show where the organizers had invited a dozen artists to live in the exhibition space for a month. The participants had built an array of tents, huts and sculpture/dwellings. I was only interested in one of them: a young Japanese artist who had reconstructed the living room from the Godard film *Contempt*. On a coffee table in front of the sofa was an assortment of Japanese magazines with articles about J.L.G. The artist was off to the side of her fake film set, seated at a table where she was making rows of small figures from white clay. I spoke with her for a little while, trying to understand the relationship between the clay figurines and the *Contempt* environment. It had something to do with "victims" and "vulnerability." She had difficult explaining, or I had some difficulty understanding, her obvious obsession with this 30-year-old French film. I knew how she felt.

I gave her my phone number and address and left.

Just remembered that when I was in Paris in 1978-79 I used to go with N.P. to see a double feature in a small movie theater off Place St. Michel in the 6th. One movie was a documentary about the Doors and the other was a short titled *Cinema n'est pas morte, Monsieur Godard.* It consisted of Patti Smith in a Paris recording studio (I may be wrong about the location) performing a song which ended in the phrase of the title. I remember nothing of the movie (in contrast to some indelible images of Jim Morrison) except her incantation "cinema n'est pas morte, Monsieur Godard." Although I didn't realize it at the time, we were watching Patti's message to Jean-Luc at exactly the moment when Godard was returning, with *Sauve Qui Peut*, to filmmaking.

It's the 1930s, in Los Angeles. A young woman whose father is involved in the film industry lands a job as an extra in a film starring Greta Garbo. The scene she appears in takes place at a race track. It's a hot summer day and everyone is wearing light clothes. At one point during a break in shooting, the young woman goes to the women's toilets where she encounters a woman standing in front of a sink with her dress pulled up, shaving her pubic hair. "Look what they're making me do, darling," Garbo says to the young woman. "They say they can see my pubic hair through the dress I'm wearing so I have to shave it off. Isn't it terrible?" Years later, the woman relishes telling the story for its shock value.

Some day I'll have to place all this Godardiana at the service of something more ambitious than a "scrapbook."

"After 40 American films, *Pierrot Le Fou* seemed extraordinary just because it had to do with thinking." (Heiner Müller, 1981)

TOO SOON, TOO SAD

Last month, even last week, I would have tried to draw a poem from this news of a distant death. Now, I potter around for an hour after the phone call, making coffee, straightening up, reading some 45-year-old essays on cinematic realism. Finally I examine, clearly but not too harshly — leave that to others, no? — my motives for that poem I'm no longer going to attempt writing (and maybe even my motives for not writing it) and I'm ready.

I'd called a friend in Barcelona about something completely unrelated (some friends of his were coming to New York and needed a place to stay). We hadn't spoken for months, although a few letters had passed back and forth. Now, as long as we were talking on the phone, he dropped this piece of news related to our lives of a dozen years ago.

I keep telling myself (at least when I remember) that every text should set out to do two things. Or, if I don't want to keep that in mind, I can put my faith in the music of the soul, as I have many times before — and as I am even now (in so far as I haven't yet thought of what second thing this text could try to do).

I was the first one to notice him: a figure that appeared in a clearing on top of the hill across the narrow valley from the old stone farmhouse in which David and his wife Elizabeth lived, and where I was a long-term guest that winter of 1982-83.

Since I finished my longish poem "In A Blue Field," (that was in September, it's November now) I've sworn to myself not to begin another text just to be able to tell myself I'm writing or just because something struck me in an immediate way. I've guess I've been struggling against two insidious forces: the Protestant work ethic (Jewish version) and perception that masquerades as inspiration.

Yesterday I should have known I wouldn't be able to hold off much longer when, waiting in a 6th Avenue diner for a friend to show up, I took out a notebook and jotted down this sentence: "Each time I decide to no longer place myself at the mercy of happenstance, something catches my eye: a woman trying to hail a cab by hurling up her red-sleeved arm like a child trying to catch a balloon floating just out of its reach . . ."

I know it's shameful that I'm thinking about Balthazar simply because he is dead, while I have barely thought about him for a moment since I was last on the island eight years ago. And really, I haven't thought about him, nor spoken to him for longer, perhaps 10 years. On the other hand, why should I have thought about him? Hundreds of people drift through our lives. After a decade, it's only a small percentage that we regularly recall.

But then I'm not really thinking about Balthazar, am I? I'm not really grappling with the story and pain of his addiction. Let's be honest: it's not Balthazar that I care about but rather the image in my mind, the resonance of a strange (or perhaps not so strange) fate that has befallen someone I once knew. What matters to me about Balthazar is his "role" — I put the word in quotes since the place was so small a one — in my life.

So, one of the two things might be: the inability of the individual to care about another person. Hard to think of anything blander to start with — at least put like that.

I can't remember whether we noticed him visually, sitting up there with his dog, or whether he was making some sound (singing? harmonica?) that attracted our attention.

I remember when we had difficulty understanding his name and I asked him to write it out and even then I couldn't tell if it was Balthazar or Balthazan. I was so ignorant of the country and language then — and still am now, because I have probably forgotten most of what I learned over those long visits throughout the 80s — that I didn't recognize the name, didn't understand that it had to be "Balthazar" because that was the name of one of the Three Magi. (I just had to look up the others: Gaspar and Melchior.)

For the first time, I think that maybe he came to that particular clearing because of us — either because he wanted to watch us or, more probably, because he wanted us to watch him.

Two months ago, when I was finishing my "elegy" for M.B. ("In a Blue Field"), I remembered that song from the early '80s (called something like "My Friends Who Died") which is built around the names of the singer's dead pals. There was something — actually a lot of things — off-putting about that record, and I hoped, when I remembered it, that I wasn't doing something similar, and I hope so again now. Is thinking about the deaths of distant acquaintances the only thing that gets me writing these days? And if so, what does that mean? Is it that the subject seems important enough to jump-start a piece of literature? Or does it have something to do with my having turned 40. Or — and this is the explanation I'd choose today — is it merely a coincidence?

He was the first real friend we made in the village. We knew people in the cafés and bars, the shops and garage, the city hall, but with Balthazar there was no financial transaction involved — he was just a young kid who wandered by with his dog one day. Actually, it took several weeks until he ventured down from the crest of the hill and across the road to our house.

Once we had established contact, he would stop by our house to chat several times a week. To an extent we took him under our wings, teaching him some English, a few chords on the guitar, facts about America. Looking back, I can see that probably everyone else in the village was too suspicious of us (a menage-à-trois — not true! — of foreigners in their late 20s who did nothing but read all day) to make friends. Balthazar was free to not so much because of his youth but because he too was an outsider, because of his mixed parentage.

I do a quick calculation: Balthazar must have not yet been 30 when he died. What were his last years like? At some point, I recall hearing, he vanished from the village. Then, later, news came that he was in some kind of rehabilitation program for addicts. Eventually, I think, he came back. I only saw him a few times after that first winter. (In the end, the friendship wasn't a very deep one.)

He was living with his grandmother. His mother was Scandinavian and his father was Mallorcan. (The only visible sign of his Nordic background — to foreign eyes at least — was that he was slightly taller than the average villager.) He had come to live with his father's mother. Her house was the last one on the edge of town on the same road that, after a five-minute walk, led past our fairly isolated residence.

What initially struck us most about him was his great love for his dog. I'm not sure I remember what kind it was. A German shepherd, maybe. This affection, which he spoke to us about, was in inescapable contrast to the way dogs were usually treated in that society. The caretaker of our house, for example, left his tied up behind the cowshed (I guess you could call it, though it was used for sheep, chickens and ducks, rather than cows). The poor animal survived on stale bread and angry kicks.

I remember Balthazar often kneeling down to throw his arms around his dog. It went everywhere with him.

I remember going to his house once. It was winter and Balthazar, his grandmother, David and I, sat around a small table in the living room. His grandmother still kept up the local tradition of filling a metal receptacle under the table with hot coals. During the visit we sat with our legs underneath the heavy tablecloth, warm in the chilly house.

I wish I remembered more. If I ever thought I'd one day be writing about Balthazar, I would have made notes or paid more attention. As it is, I can only speculate about the pain and confusion that was there waiting for drugs to dissolve.

For one second, I conceive of a project: I'll go back to the town of Olara and start a personal investigation. I'll interview everyone who knew Balthazar, find out what happened to him, write an exhaustive and harrowing account of the short and unhappy life of a Spanish youth.

Why would I want to do such a thing? Well, at least it would be a chance for me to know, for once in my life, the full circumstances behind a tragedy. (Reason? Since my parents' marriage fell apart when I was about 12, I haven't been inclined to seek out the details of people's private troubles.) It would also get me away from this desk, away from this computer, away from "literature."

But I really have no desire to escape from any of these things: on the contrary, the challenge is to stay close to them, at least for a few hours every Saturday and Sunday.

Communicating with Balthazar was a problem. He spoke little English, I spoke almost no Spanish, and no Mallorquin. As I recall, we communicated in a mixture of English, Spanish and French. It was primitive but sufficient.

At this point, I can't even say with any certainty what we spoke about. Music, probably. Let this loss of memory be emblematic of Balthazar's loss: solitary, without achievement, dead at an early age after nothing more than some years of squalor and chaos. I think (out of realism and not self-importance) of these pages (by someone who barely knew him, and has so little to recall) being finally the only mark Balthazar has left on the world.

But I immediately tell myself: perhaps he had a wife, a child, a circle of friends whose mourning continues and resonates — more deeply than these pages by a distant writer who never tried to save anyone's life.

And now the urge to transmute all this (and whatever other scraps I can dredge up) into a poem begins to make itself felt, like waves of sleepiness. (I guess I'm ready for what E. would call a "synthetic act" — like Manzoni's *Merda d'artista*.)

As I write this paragraph, it's a sunny autumn Sunday afternoon. I'm sitting at my computer in front of the window that overlooks Canal Street, which is now filling up with traffic for the Holland Tunnel. The first Clash album is on the Walkman. I am letting my body sway slightly to the rhythm of "Police and Thieves." I am aware of the great luxury of all this, especially the feeling of safety with which I write.

After a death like Balthazar's, everyone who knew him wonders whether he would have survived if they had done more to help him.

As long as I keep this music blasting in my ears, I'm not going to be able to accomplish anything of any literary value. What's the point of preparing myself with a dozen pages of Francis Ponge if I wipe them out with a half hour of the Clash? But I'm afraid that if I take off the headphones, I won't be able to write at all on this subject.

I've turned off the music, at least for a few minutes.

Survival is a matter of elation and guilt, and guilt at the elation.

Did that tree a block away lose its leaves without me noticing or was it already dead before fall came?

I can't reconcile the image of that boy wandering with his dog around the terraced hillsides of a Mediterranean island, like something out of an old tale or poem, with the circumstances of his death. David said his body had been found in a public toilet in the city of Palma.

But we all, or many of us, travel far from where we begin. Every war criminal was once a little boy.

I imagine that, like a slashing guitar chord, each hit of smack is a surge of revenge against everyone and everything who has wronged you in life, and what's more, it makes you feel so good at the same time as it uses your body and life as surrogate victim.

(As you might guess, I've turned the music on again. Still the Clash: *Give 'Em Enough Rope*.)

So, am I going to write about the various drug addicts I've known?

No, what I want to remember are those days, also autumn, as I recall (music off) when David, Elizabeth and I seemed to have escaped from America and all her hypnotic glitz into a world still governed by seasons and religion, where silent youths wandered down from hills as if out of Greek lyrics.

In another decade, would Balthazar simply have drunk himself to death instead?

In my mind, his death is also the death of the world we found in that village nestled at the foot of the island's mountains.

Death always seem an exception, and it is — if only because it takes up so little of each life.

Am I supposed to keep sitting here until I figure something out? What is it that I think is suddenly going to become beautifully clear?

I just want someone to hear the tiny sound made by a single person going under, too soon, too sad.

That's what I might have engraved on his tombstone, if it were up to me, if he had one (I don't know):

Too soon, too sad

O.K., turn the music back on.

A LOST PROFILE

As usual on Sunday morning, I'm flipping through the "Arts & Leisure" section of the *New York Times*, looking to see if, somewhere among the giant ads for would-be blockbuster movies, there's an article I feel like reading. If I'm lucky, I'll find an interesting piece — framed by images of fireballs, muscular killers and leggy blondes — about the latest Hong Kong auteur, or maybe it will be a piece about how some young American novelist is unexpectedly assisting a legendary European director to make a successful comeback. In the mood for media-industry updates and human-interest stories from the cultural front, the last thing I expect is to be confronted with something that might pertain to me personally. After all, if that was what I wanted, I wouldn't be reading the *Times*, would I?

What changes this is a photograph on one of the music pages ("pop/jazz"). It's a shot centered on a singer in the midst of a chaotic performance. With a look of agony on his face, as if he's just been shot or stabbed, he seems to be falling from the small stage into the audience. Someone (a woman, I think) is pushing her arm straight into his chest. She could be trying to keep him from toppling over, or protecting herself from his imminent attack or simply trying to touch him in the time-honored tradition of pop star adulation. Pop star? He looks more like a bit player — lightweight boxer, small-time hood — from a '50s crime movie. He could be Elisha J. Cook's grandson.

I instantly recognize the singer and the venue, even though I've never seen this particular image before. The scene is so familiar that I don't have to look at the caption to identify the subject but when I do so, automatically, like any trained newspaper reader, this is what I see: "James Chance, above, singing with his No Wave band the Contortions at Max's Kansas City in Manhattan in the mid-1970s."

Shot with a flash and sharply tilted, the photograph is neatly divided in two. To the right of the singer are the front rows of the audience. I can see four ordinary looking men in their 20s and a few women of the same age, all of them jumbled together at narrow tables extending perpendicularly from the low stage. Except for one man looking at the camera (in any crowd shot there's always one person who insists on making eye contact with the camera lens), everyone is focused on the singer, who is standing (thanks to that outstretched arm) a little left of center, microphone in one hand, his big mouth open wide. In the background, some distance from the singer, is the band, silhouetted against a darkness broken only by an illuminated exit sign and a few barely visible ceiling lights. In the lower left-hand corner, anchoring the whole composition, is the face in profile of one spectator. I can't help noticing, at some point in my perusal of the image, that everyone in the picture is white.

I compare the photograph and the caption. "Mid-1970s" is wrong. I'm sure this shot was taken sometime between 1978 and 1980. Most likely in 1979, the year I often went to see the Contortions.

My eyes linger on the singer for a little while (keep in mind that everything I'm describing occurs within a few seconds, as long as it takes to read one or two of these sentences), remembering how he looked and the visceral drama of his performances. My gaze searches out the visible musicians in the darkness behind the singer. To the left there's a guitarist wearing a white shirt and narrow dark tie (his electric guitar repeats this high-contrast look). To the right of the singer is another guitarist, a wraithlike woman in black, with chopped-off blonde hair and a long throat rising from her black-sheathed body. My eyes drop to the audience who, I now note, look conventional and collegiate, showing no trace of the band's edgy retro look. Did I also look like a jock or nerd when I used to go to Max's to see the Contortions? Surely not. (I begin — and quickly abandon — the task of mentally cataloguing my wardrobe circa 1979: it's impossible to recall a single piece of clothing I might have worn.) Is this dichotomy between the musicians and the audience typical of a Contortions performance at Max's, or did the photographer just happen to catch what seem to be a few carloads of New England college students making the downtown scene? As one part of my mind is trying to guess at the accuracy of this glimpse into a past which I never expected to be shown again, or at least not just now, I direct my eyes out of the photo and up to the beginning of the article, which, I now realize, it is time to read. But as I visually glide out of the photo, I look again at the guy in the lower left-hand corner. With my attention focused on the drama of the singer's imminent plunge into the audience, I had hardly noticed this profile before, but now it suddenly jumps out at me in a moment of strange metamorphosis. The features of the young man snap out of anonymity into a face I can identify.

It's me.

I stare at the photograph, at that profile caught 17 years ago in a split second of flashed light. It can't be me. I was already amazed to find a photograph of the Contortions at Max's unfolding in front of me, but that the photograph should also include me in it is really unbelievable.

As I begin to believe it, a feeling of happiness comes over me. I'm happy and — it takes me a moment to identify the feeling — grateful. I feel so indescribably full and content that I have to turn away and draw a deep breath. Then I look again, with increased wonder, at the photo.

So this is what I looked like at a club in 1979. So this is the person that, all those years ago, was me. To see an image of myself in the midst of that long-gone world feels like one of the most miraculous things that has ever happened to me. Here, completely unexpectedly, is proof that I didn't dream that life, proof that I really was around for No Wave — that, as the Times puts it, "brief and localized movement that resisted wholesale absorption into mainstream culture." Yes, there I am.

Or am I?

I look more closely and suddenly start to feel a little doubtful. Am I really sure that it's me? Like a camera refocusing, I adjust my vision and now the profiled face doesn't look like me at all. The nose is too pointed. The eyes (or at least the one I can see) are the wrong shape. That doesn't look like the kind of haircut I had in 1979. The face that a minute before was mine now threatens to change back into that of a stranger.

The happiness and gratitude ebb away, but I'm not yet sure it's not me.

I need a second opinion, the eyes of some other reader who might recognize this profile. Perhaps even now one of my friends has identified me, and is picking up the telephone to call. Or maybe it's up to me to call. But whom? When no one comes to mind, I realize that I'm not ready to involve any of my friends in this predicament. Instead, I think about contacting the photographer — her name, which I recognize, is given under the picture in tiny print — and asking if I could see any other photographs she shot that night. Surely there is a roll, or even several, from which a photo editor had chosen the image that happens to have a profile of that young man in the lower right-hand corner. In another photo there might be a view from a different angle that would show a face I could be more certain was my own. Or one that included some item of clothing I could remember owning. A shot that showed a friend sitting next to "me" would also help.

It's a little absurd not to be able to recognize yourself. Part of the reason I can't be sure is because it's a profile shot and, like most people, I have rarely seen my own face in profile. I'm also having trouble because I think the person in the photo looks so ugly. I think I want to resist admitting that this is me, even though I want so much to believe that I was at Max's that night, sitting close to the stage, and that the photographer caught me and that my image is in the "Arts & Leisure" section of the *New York Times*, because I don't want to have to incorporate that face into my memories — such as they are — of those years.

Thankfully, as I keep looking, he starts to seem less actively unattractive. But, I must still admit, he really does look strange, especially in relation to the other faces in the audience, who all can fit into some conventional American physiognomic type.

There could be a positive side to this. Maybe the "ugliness" and "strangeness" is more proof that it's me. What I'm experiencing could be a reflexive reaction, as when you hear a recording of your voice and fail to "recognize" it because it sounds nothing like the voice you are accustomed to hear reverberating in your own head. Would any of the other people pictured in this photo, if they happened to open the *Sunday Times* and saw this 16-year-old photo, find themselves equally strange looking?

As I ponder this, another reaction to the photo rolls over me: a sense of absurdity that the dazed-looking guy just off-center from this "historic moment" (or at least someone who might be him) should find himself, 16 years later, writing about the photograph someone happened to take of it.

Objectively, I can see that this is an interesting photograph. As such, it's not unthinkable that someone should write about it. What's absurd is that someone who is in the picture (maybe) should be the one writing about it. Imagine one of the three men in August Sander's *Peasants Going to a Dance* writing an essay years later about that photograph. Or one of the hard-pressed revelers in Brassai's nightlife photographs of the 1930s penning a story based on his image. Unless they are public figures, we expect the people in photographs to be silent. Why? Because we don't want to imagine them conscious of our own eventual gaze?

Like those well-known images, this is a strong composition, especially because of that one arm, in a white shirt sleeve rolled above the elbow, jammed into the stomach of the singer, whose grimace and collapsing body are reminiscent of Lee Harvey Oswald at the moment Jack Ruby shot him. The late '50s/early '60s style suit, cut from a shiny fabric chosen by the singer no doubt to evoke the outfits of early James Brown, subtly reinforces this association. The composition is also striking for the way the singer simultaneously divides both the right and left sides of the photograph (the audience and "me") and the foreground and background (the audience and "me" versus the band and the darkness behind them).

Looking at the grimace on the singer's face, I remember listening to a friend theorize about James Chance's importance at that moment. Punk was fading away, I recall him explaining, and the whole survival of the music scene in New York or, at any rate, the chance of moving to the next phase, had come to rest on Chance's shoulders. He alone had to sustain the edge of music, keep it dangerous. This is what necessitated the violence, the way he leaped out into the audience — as he is about to do in the photo — and started fights or fell to the floor while continuing to let out the hoarse shouts that marked his singing style. (He also played saxophone, only slightly less aggressively.) It was the same friend who warned me, the first time I went to hear the Contortions with him, not to get too close to the stage.

If this is me in the photo, I must have eventually grown brave enough to sit close to the stage. Though I'm also off to the side, less exposed to the performer's theatrical fury than the people in the center. Is this cautious position another piece of evidence, however small, in my attempt to prove (at least to myself) that this is (or at least was) me?

Why do I want to prove this? I mean apart from the two most obvious reasons: that I would be pleased to be shown present at a now apparently legendary underground event; that this sliver of my past has been rescued, and inserted into official history.

Two of the band members are not identified, but I know who they are, and I can easily name them, even though they're hardly visible, even after so many years. The line-up that night would have been, from left to right as this photo shows them, Jody Harris (guitar), Don Christiansen (drums), James Chance (vocals and sax), James Honeyman Scott (bass), Pat Place (guitar). Actually the bass player and drummer aren't visible, but I can see the drum kit and the neck of the bass guitar so I know they must have been there. And maybe I should add Adele Bertei on keyboards, or had she already left the group? There's someone on stage partly hidden by Chance that might be her. It's funny that I'm far more certain about the presence of the invisible-drummer and bass player, than I am about my own presence.

If in the end this turns out not to be me, am I going to feel ridiculous for writing these pages about a photograph which has nothing to do with me? But if it isn't me, who is it?

I now notice that this person, who may or may not be me, is not looking at the singer. Rather than focusing on the violent action happening just two or three feet away, he is looking at something else equally close: the blonde woman whose face is almost completely turned away from the camera, in a beautiful example of profile perdu. This sets up an interesting geometry of gazes: in the photograph we see his (my?) profile, as he (me?) looks at the profile of a women we cannot see. (She is looking, I can only assume raptly, at the singer.)

What's going on here? Did he come with the blonde woman? Or has he just noticed her, amid the mayhem and noise? Now that I notice what he's looking at, I also see that the young-man-in-profile's expression is one of awestruck lovesickness.

The woman is wearing a luxuriantly fluffy, expensive looking sweater. Her thick hair is pulled back and then cascades down her back, here and there reflecting the light of the flashbulb like polished metal. It looks even richer and more luxurious then her sweater — surely a conscious fashion choice on her part. Did I know anyone who would have fit her description, who had hair like that and wore fluffy sweaters? And would I have gone with them to Max's to see the Contortions? No even remotely likely candidate comes to mind, though in a period of my life so intent on sensation and oblivion, that's not surprising.

There's so much that's not available in the photograph. I can remember the Contortions, I can remember going to Max's, but I can't recall the photo being taken (why should I?) or the blonde woman (who maybe I didn't even know but just happened to find myself sitting near). If she was in fact someone I knew, I'd like to know what happened to her. And also what happened to that emotion visible on "my" face. And what happened to the world inside the head of that young man with the hangdog, lovesick expression. The most important thing the photograph tells me, I now begin to realize, is not that I was at Max's to see the Contortions that night or that this is what I looked like circa 1979, but that almost nothing remains of my life at that moment. I'm feeling less happy and grateful.

I take another look at the nerdish, jockish guys in the audience. I look at "me" again, at the haircut I may or may not have had in 1979. Thank god it's hipper — very short on the sides, kind of a mess in front — than theirs. (I say this not just for my potential sake but also and more importantly because this one, not particularly successful haircut at least saves James Chance in this photo from performing for a completely square crowd.) In the end it's ridiculous how much seems to boil down to a choice of haircuts. And this is precisely the nuance that is first lost. Or maybe I'm wrong. Maybe this is the only thing that survives, a stylistic differentiation, rather than the deeper necessity, the impulse to do something back at life in a way that could restore the balance that one dimly remembered once having had, and to do so in a form that brought attention, love and (if you were wildly lucky) money your way.

I'm trying to explain why I was there — I mean why I would have been there, why I may have been there. There was a purity to that band that set it apart from so many others in those years of musical turmoil.

I'm also trying to think of the painter who could best do justice to this scene. Francis Bacon? Franz Kline? Some Italian Baroque master who excelled at Deposition scenes?

I try to picture myself showing the article to a friend and asking if, in his or her opinion, the face in the lower left-hand corner could be mine. Or maybe I shouldn't tell them so much? Just hand them the article and ask if they notice anything interesting about the photograph.

I won't do it. It's too absurd and this photograph already means too much to me to reduce it to a show-and-tell item. What I will do, when my wife comes back from the trip she's on, is show the picture to her and ask her if she thinks it's me. I guess that she's the only one who I'm not embarrassed in front of. Or is it that I share everything important with her and that this is important and, therefore, must be shared?

Is it important?

I'm in no rush for a second opinion, because if the person I show it to says no, and I believe them, these pages will come to an end. And if their answer is yes? If they say, "of course it's you"? The result will probably be the same. Only as long as I'm uncertain can I keep working on these pages, only as long as I don't arrive at a definitive self-recognition can I keep writing this commentary to Marcia Resnick's photograph that can be found, should anyone be interested, on page 24 of the Arts & Leisure section of the *New York Times*, September 1, 1996.

A CAMEO

I'm on my bicycle. It's Sunday, *Domenica*, I'm heading home from buying a newspaper at a bookstore on the Via Manzoni and an image is stuck in my head.

The photograph shows the founder of the bookstore, Gianfranco Monferrato, posing with Alfred Hitchcock. In the large black-and-white print displayed by itself behind the semi-circular counter which holds both the cash register and stacks of national and local newspapers, the film director is seated while the bookstore owner/publisher (Monferrato is also a prominent publishing house) is leaning towards him. Hitchcock holds an Italian translation, published by Monferrato, of one of his popular mystery anthologies. In the picture Monferrato's bushy moustache and eyebrows and heavy glasses suggest a Groucho Marx impersonator more than a successful publisher and scion of a great fortune. (The bookstore and publishing house, while successful in their own right, were originally financed with a small portion of the vast wealth Monferrato had inherited.) But in fact the man in the photo is neither a fake-Groucho nor a publisher/bookstore owner nor a wealthy scion — history remembers him as a suicidal terrorist.

In a month it will be 20 years since Gianfranco Monferrato blew himself up while trying to plant a bomb near an electric pylon in a nearby suburb. Ironically, one of his best-known publishing ventures were two volumes about 1960s urban guerillas in South America which became handbooks for fanatical leftist terrorists in the 1970s. (How good, one can't help wondering, were the instructions on bomb-making in those two volumes?) But I'm not about to start reviewing radical politics of the 1960s and 1970s; my only concern today is that double portrait of Monferrato and Hitchcock.

Alfred Hitchcock is known for a number of things, that is, his reputation as a film director can be broken down into a series of separate, interrelated parts which, brought together again, constitute the Hitchcock myth. These include, in no particular order:

1. He always appeared in his own movies at least once, but only as an extra in the crowd, never as a protagonist.

2. His films are often about an innocent man wrongly accused who must flee the authorities while at the same time he pursues the villains whose exposure and capture is his only hope of exoneration.

3. He had a thing for icy blondes like Kim Novak, Grace Kelly, Ingrid Bergman.

4. *The Birds*, perhaps his best-known movie, depicts the attempted destruction of society by thousands of small creatures working in concert.

5. He planned out each film perfectly before it was shot and famously declared that his own presence on the set was wholly superfluous.

6. He was fat.

As I roll along, the Saturday-Sunday *Herald Trib* in my basket, my jacket half-open, the juxtaposition of Monferrato and Hitchcock, and the prominent place accorded that juxtaposition in the flagship Monferrato store, refuses to leave my mind. Hoping for some flash of understanding, I start matching up aspects of Monferrato with those of Hitchcock:

1. In the confusing political landscape of the late 1960s and early 1970s, Gianfranco Monferrato's entrance into the world of the books he liked to publish was a walk-on part that got out of hand; where most people in his situation would have been content with making a cameo appearance, he wanted a speaking part.

2. Monferrato decided to go underground prior to being suspected of any crime, he was thus an innocent man on the run, and even if he did commit crimes before March 1972 (when the bomb went off) he did so in the service of the "revolution," to protect his country from the right wing coup he was convinced to be imminent.

3. G.M. was planting his bomb at the foot of a tall structure of cold metal at whose summit there might have been a crackle of electric current.

4. The birds in Hitchcock's film are, in their own way, model terrorists, showing little concern for human life as they attempt a methodical takeover of society.

5. & 6. These cancel each other out: Hitch was the perfect film-

maker, a flawless artist, yet in real life he was grossly overweight, the opposite of his cinematic efficiency. G.M. set out to commit a crime, to become a character in a Hitchcock film while also executing a scenario with the efficiency of the great director himself. He wanted to conquer the tall blonde, to unleash the attack of his fellow conspirators, yet he did not grasp his correlation to the real-life Hitchcock whose obesity clearly ruled anything more than a "waddle-on" part in his own films. They would never be men of action, only the men who called out "action." Hitchcock knew this perfectly well; it was G.M.'s fatal mistake not to recognize such discrepancies.

Hitchcock used to tell a story about his film version of Joseph Conrad's *The Secret Agent*, a novel concerning late-19th-century European terrorists. In the film a small boy is unknowingly given a bomb to carry across London. The camera follows him sitting innocently on a slow bus (heavy traffic has delayed it) as we, the audience, know the package in his lap is ticking away. In the film, as in the book, the bomb eventually explodes, killing the boy and his fellow passengers. Hitchcock said he learned a terrible lesson from this film, which was a commercial flop. The lesson, which he never forgot, was that in any such situation, when the audience has been brought to the edge of their seats with anxiety, the anticipated event must never occur, the bomb must never ever actually go off. If it does, Hitchcock realized, the audience will never forgive the director and the film will fail.

Surely, I think, as I wheel my bicycle into the courtyard of where I live, it was all these things which the photograph was trying to say. Why else would it be there, the only visible memorial to the store's founder and namesake? Or am I looking for mysteries, for hidden meanings, where there are none? Am I like those obsessive conspiracy theorists who insist on seeing Monferrato's death as the result of a government plot? (And like those equally obsessive academics who write massive theses on the symbolism and auto-referentiality of Hitchcock's movies.) That photograph could be nothing more than a sign of Monferrato's passion for film. For all I know he was an avid Hitchcock fan. The truth is, his heirs probably chose that particular image because it showed Monferrato in a humorous, carefree mood, at complete odds with the image of an inept idealist, a wealthy man playing with dangerous toys, continually insisted on by the Italian right.

I lock my bike and race up to the apartment, impatient for news and coffee. Enough of Monferrato. I'm not going to solve this particular mystery today. And why should I? Isn't it supposed to be the day of rest? As if on cue, I hear bells start to ring as Mass lets out somewhere nearby.

I decide, during what's left of this peaceful Sunday morning, that things are as they appear. Looking at the photo ("the city of Vukovar after heavy bombardment") on the front page, that other image starts to fade from my mind. I wonder if I was perhaps the only person in the world thinking of Monferrato today? I try to hold on, for a last moment, to the mirrored destinies I thought I saw in that blurring black-and-white image. For a moment, two faces superimposed, then none.

14 THINGS

(for Elena Berriolo)

The angle at which I intersect with them
can't be described in degrees.
It's a measure of
(I close my eyes and listen
to the cottony buzz of mid-afternoon traffic,
remember some lines scolding a miserable novelist's latest effort
in this morning's book review,
open them and look at one of the 14 objects in front of me)
need and need of distance.

1. A painting on board, approx. 2 by 3 feet, of a man smoking a pipe. Dressed in a green suit and white shirt (no tie, collar unbuttoned to show undershirt), the figure sits in an old-fashioned office chair with his feet up on the desk in a pose which suggests both relaxation and thoughtfulness. Behind him a couple of abstract paintings hang on the wall and there is a bookshelf loaded with thick volumes. Full of clumsy proportion but with an undeniable presence, the painting seems to be the work of a talented amateur and, as far as I'm concerned, well worth the $5 I paid for it in a "junk barn" in upstate New York about 10 years ago.

What is the man thinking about? The past? present? future? It would help if we knew what his present was. The amateurishness of the painting makes it harder to date than if it were the work of a professional artist. The furniture and the figure's clothes and haircut suggest the late 1940s, but the Mondrian-like paintings on the wall strike me as too advanced for the work of an amateur artist of that time. Shall we say mid-1950s? That would mean the painting was made about the time I was born.

It was in the same region of New York State, on another summer weekend, that a friend of mine gave me a 1920s lamp decorated with

American Indian motifs. We drove back to the house where we were staying and when our host saw me walk in with the lamp she gave it a horrified look. "It's ugly and dirty. I can't stand anything like that in my house," she said to me, nearly screaming. Trying to be a good guest, I took the lamp to the porch, but this was not good enough since, as our host pointed out, she would still see it every time she went in or out. She didn't say "that lamp's evil vibrations will seep through the walls," but I could see she was thinking something of the kind. I transferred the poor lamp to the trunk of a car.

Although I realized (if not before, certainly right then) that my host was mentally unstable and not fully accountable for her actions, I was nonetheless furious with her for by now I had totally identified with the lamp. To call it "ugly and dirty" was tantamount to calling me those things. I didn't show my anger but resolved that as soon as I could get away from that house (with my lamp), I would try to stay clear of the woman.

A dozen years later I still have the lamp, but my wife hates it passionately and we've banished it to the storage room, along with other things deemed too valuable to toss out but not valuable enough to bother selling.

I would like those 14 objects to somehow appear on this page without description. I've always dreamed of inventing a form of writing which would short-circuit description, of finding a way to present something that would be as easy as turning on a tape recorder or a video camera.

The real problem is that (at my job as an art critic and editor of an art magazine) I've spent all week describing objects hanging on walls or standing in museums and galleries — or improving other people's descriptions of such objects — so that to do that here is unbearable. Just mentioning the possibility of describing something (even if it's not a painting, sculpture or installation) has my eyelids flopping down in fatigue.

But am I really tired or is the fatigue a sign of something?

The horns of backed-up traffic erupt, a helicopter echoes over the river, E.'s iron slides across the worn fabric of a tablecloth that once belonged to my grandparents or hers (I can't tell from this far away).

What will keep me awake at times like this? **Changing the font of my text? CHANGING IT AGAIN?** *And again?* Perhaps I could fall back on my favorite procedure of reading my peers' books on the lookout for artistic missteps that will allow me to close the volume and relegate the author to the category of "ones I don't have to worry about any more." Also useful to sustain a semblance of inspiration are recordings by any of the following: Stereolab, Saint-Etienne, Pizzicato Five.

Was it in '92 or '93 that Adrian D. and I found ourselves in the French city of Saint-Etienne to write about a show at a local museum? I was content to review the show but Adrian, ever the enterprising journalist, made the most of the visit by also wangling an interview with the mayor of St.-Etienne in order to — at first I thought Adrian was kidding when he told me his idea — get his opinion of the successful English pop group which had named itself after his city. It was on that occasion, in nearby Lyon, that I found a book whose title translates as *Ornament of an Interior Death*.

2. a painting by my father. On an 8-by-10-inch piece of canvas board, it shows the head of a bearded man against a green background. The brown hair and beard form a single mass. The figure is placed slightly off-center and leans to the left. The style is suggestive of an Italian Primitive, partly because of the golden color of the figure's skin. The nose is long and thin, almost knifelike; the eyes small and green.

For years this painting hung in the house of old family friends (Joe & Sylvia G.). Joe once told me he'd titled it *Habakkuk* because it was such a small painting and Habakkuk was the shortest book of the Old Testament. (Being a rabbi, Joe would know.)

I just took the painting off the wall. There's a yellowed slip of paper taped to the back (by address stickers with J. & S.'s address in San Jose) on which is typed "Habbakuk by J. Rubinstein" and "please return to Consuelo Howatt" (my mother). There are addresses after both their names which I recognize as their respective parents' houses. Also typed on the label, which is coming off, is the information "not for sale."

I surmise that my parents were not married when *Habbakuk* was painted; that it was in a show; that instead of selling it, they gave it to

S. & J. Then, as so often before, as so often in the future, I quickly come to the end of my knowledge of family history, except the knowledge that everyone I would like to ask is dead. Here we are: ignorant me and this dusty little painting in its wood frame painted a dusky gold.

Between this paragraph and the previous one, I just read the book of Habakkuk, learning first of all that it is misspelled on my father's painting (it should have one b and two k's). Less than two pages long, it's filled with images of violence and destruction, promises to obey the Lord and, at the end, a few lines denouncing graven images. According to the *Macmillan Encyclopedia of Judaism*, Habakkuk "deals at length with the problem of injustice in the world." Reading this, I think immediately of my father's last words to me, whispered from his hospital bed the day before his 55-year-old heart finally gave out after 3 days of struggle. "Try to dispense a sense of justice in the world," he told his 17-year-old only son and heir.

I look at *Habbakuk* (the painting) and then at the $5 painting of #1 and think how perhaps the artist's son or daughter would be as glad to have that portrait as I am to have *Habakkuk*. Perhaps it's a missing piece of their family history, a relic of their father's or mother's artistic youth. Am I uneasy with owning something with a history that pertains to strangers? Is that what bothers me? Behind this am I unconsciously experiencing that common fear that one day my most precious possessions will end up in an upstate "junk barn"?

The arbitrary subject remains an effective weapon to use against convention, sentimentality, self-importance and other such afflictions of "serious" writing. I've learned from Roussel and Breton how to focus on an apparently random piece of the world — the label on a bottle of mineral water, a strange object picked up at a flea market — and derive illumination from it. But, at the other extreme (all the while staying within the realm of 20th-century French poetry) is Francis Ponge, who chose his subjects (objects) with supreme deliberation. Of course, he has his own very effective means of keeping "the poetic" at bay, without having to turn to the arbitrary.

In any case, I am no longer happy with choosing to focus a text on something that means nothing to me.

I'm thinking about such things because I was just leafing through Clark Coolidge's *The Crystal Text* (a book I've still not read more than a page of continuously) and wondering what sort of object I would choose if I were going to write at such length on a single subject. And then I looked around me and realized that I was looking at some of the objects I am writing about, 12 of which remain to be mentioned.

3. a postcard of a painting — 18th century, I'll guess, resisting for a moment the temptation to turn it over — of a young woman holding a parasol over the head of an older woman who is seated and leaning on a cane. Or maybe it's an old man. The young woman is dressed in an extravagant orange silk dress. Floating behind her is a crinkly piece of bright yellow and white fabric that curves under her left arm (which rests on a basket of fruit) and into the foreground. Both figures are silhouetted against a mass of very dark trees — really more like black smoke than foliage — and above a bit of clouds and sky and sun. What I enjoy about the image, apart from the décolleté of the woman in orange, is the light caught (or perhaps emanating from) the golden fabric strangely floating behind her and the dramatic negative space around these almost cut-out figures.

I allow myself to read the back of the card. The painting, dated 1710-1720, is by Jean Ranc (1674-1735), an artist I've never heard of before. The title is *Vertumme et Pomone*, words (names?) which likewise mean nothing to me. It measures 170 by 120 centimeters (about 5 1/2 by 4 feet), is painted with oil on canvas, from the collection of the Musée Fabre, Montpellier, and was included in the exhibition "Les Amours des Dieux" at the Grand Palais in Paris in 1991 where I saw it and where I bought this postcard, which I will now put back on the wall.

One day a man receives a postcard thanking him for a wonderful night. It is signed with a woman's name. He doesn't recognize the name, nor the address the sender has included on the card. He has no memory of any recent evening with a woman which might have inspired the postcard. Intrigued, he gets in his car and drives to the address. (The date is the late 1940s, the place a city in Northern California, so you must imagine the appropriate cars and clothing.) Like a detective, he sits in his car watching the house. He sits there for a long time, trying to remember, trying to get up the courage to get out of his car, walk across the street and ring the doorbell. Who is the woman? What does she look like? Is this a trick of some kind? Is he ready to risk changing his life?

Eventually, he starts the car and slowly drives away. The mystery remains a mystery but he remembers it vividly enough to one day tell it to his son, who nurses the anecdote for 25 years before being compelled to write it down for reasons he isn't quite ready to understand.

What shall we imagine was on the postcard?

4. The magazine's matte not glossy cover has a brushy ink drawing of a city street — the composition is reminiscent of O'Keeffe's views of lower Manhattan's canyons — surrounded by a wide border the color of dried blood. It's called *The Downtown Review*. Date: Fall/Winter 79/80. Price $3.50. I can't remember buying it — and why should I, after 17 years? — and I don't recognize any of the contributors' names. When I say "don't recognize," I mean that there is no one I was aware of then and no one that I've met or even heard of since. It's a little sad to read the names of these young writers knowing that 17 years later they will still not have achieved the recognition of which they no doubt dreamed.

The magazine includes the transcript of a long panel discussion on painting which I still find pretty interesting. There are also pieces on film, dance, music and a handful of poems. *The Downtown Review* doesn't seem to represent any particular esthetic — part of its problem? — but it does remind me that I grew up in a time when "artistic creativity" was considered to be practically a birthright. We were raised and educated to think of ourselves as little geniuses, as a nation of Picassos and Hemingways, notions encouraged by the period's easy affluence and obsession with liberation in every form. Not for us dreams of wealth, discovery or heroism: we would all be painters or poets or dancers or musicians. Maybe that's why I hold on to this review, as a poignant reminder of my generation's unquestioning faith in the value of artistic creation.

At the time I planned to found a magazine of my own. One day in 1980, I invited my friends M. and J. over to my $250-a-month loft in Tribeca. The only furniture in the large space was a bed, a chair and one of those wooden cylinders used to roll wire on — I can't remember what they're called. Using plastic milk crates and wooden boards I made some benches for the three of us to sit on and put the wooden cylinder in the middle as a makeshift coffee table.

The reason for the meeting was to talk about my idea to start a literary review, each issue of which would be devoted to a single writer. I hoped that M. and J. would join me. I had copies of two French periodicals with formats similar to what I had in mind: *L'Arc* (issues on Perec, Cortazar, Francis Bacon) and *L'Herne* (a Karl Kraus number). They looked at the magazines, though I seem to remember that neither knew much French. We discussed the project for several hours, considering possible subjects and contributors. My friends seemed interested but I somehow knew they would never really do anything about it. I wasn't much better. That "meeting" was the most I ever did toward realizing my idea, apart from making lists of potential subjects (I remember considering Henry Green, Laura Riding and Harry Mathews). A year later, as I drifted further away from such academic concerns, I'd pretty much forgotten the project and both my prospective collaborators had become heroin addicts.

It's such a brittle word, "fourteen." I remember being 14 as also somehow brittle. At that age, I was at a hippie prep school in rural northern California. It was 1969. My mother had died a year and a half earlier and my father and I had moved to San Francisco. After seeing me miserable at my big-city, public junior high, he had tightened his financial belt and enrolled me in this boarding school. I started growing my hair long and discovered marijuana and LSD and entered into several years of misery at my inability to procure a girlfriend.

Sonnets have 14 lines. Like this one:

"Equation"

Fate, these walls and I
Conspire a holy trinity.
The screens keep out the flies
no more than you measure infinity.
Nightly God's respiration
Echoes dumb marble corridor
Embarrassing Michael
dressed like a picador.

God woos his charges à la mode
Preaches them in Coptic ode
Rails at them in cryptic code
Pricks at them with faithless goad.

He harries them from pillar to post
He sets upon them frightening ghost.

Here's another one (translated from Spanish, badly)

"Why"

Why do you weep as you write? Your letter
has marks of burning tears
which without doubt will fall on the page
like a magnificent string of diamonds.

Now ungrateful luck separates us,
but don't cry anymore, lovely one, I beg you;
Eventually, bliss and peace will arrive
in this life satiated with wounds.

Together some day, no more apart,
your sorrows will be illusory myths
and love will bring us constant joys

If you return to crying for necessary sorrows,
dry your loving tears
with the infinite kisses of my lips.

The first sonnet was written by my father and published in a chapbook my uncle printed in 1942. My father was 24 that year and about to enlist in the U.S. Army. As far as I know, the 16 poems in the pamphlet (it's called *Se*, a nice bilingual pun) are the only ones he ever published.

The author of the second is my great-grandfather, Pedro Ulloa, who published hundreds of poems in various Mexican newspapers in the early part of the century. He died in 1923 and years after his death, one of his children collected his poems in a privately published volume from which I've translated "Porqué?"

My Spanish is inadequate to do more than achieve a shaky approximation of his verse. I can't even tell if he was any good as a poet. My aunt always downplays his writing, describing him as nothing more than a provincial versifier. I'm not so sure. There seems to be an interesting mixture of symbolist imagery, political pronouncements, local history and romantic sentiment in his poems. Sometimes I like to think that he's an undiscovered genius and that I should get his poems translated properly into English and promote his discovery. The only problem is that I've never really read his poems. I've made it through a handful of shorter ones, with frequent recourse to the dictionary but about most of his work I remain in the dark.

I'm a pretty poor custodian of the family legacy. Now that almost everyone from the previous generation who knew his work is dead, I suppose I feel the responsibility weighing more heavily upon me, but what can I do? I'm not even a very good custodian of my own sonnets, judging by the hundreds of unpublished poems in boxes, notebooks and computer disks.

As for my father's poem, I can't get too enthusiastic about it. The meter is a mess, the tone is shaky and the meaning is too oblique for me to decipher.

Somewhere, I've got a sheaf of poems my mother wrote in college. If I can find them and there's a sonnet among them, I'll add it to these pages.

I decide to find out something about Vertumme and Pomone. First I try the *Larousse Dictionnaire Complet illustré* (1908 edition), which tells me that Vertumne is a Roman divinity of Etruscan origin who presided over the seasons. Pomone is identified simply as the goddess of fruits. I try the *New Columbia Encyclopedia* (4th edition, 1975). Nothing for either name nor anything resembling them, but I do notice an entry for the Southern California city of Pomona (incorporated 1888) where, the NCE tells me, "citrus fruits and vegetables are canned and shipped." Hmm, could there be a connection there? Looking in the *American Heritage Dictionary* (edition unknown to me because the title page has been partly ripped out), I notice that Pomona is also the name of one of the Orkney Islands. (For a time I believed that my Scottish ancestors had come from the Orkneys, but I recently came on a document linking James Howatt, my forbear who arrived on Prince Edward Island in 1769, to the town of Lockerbie in the lowlands.) All the other Orkneys have Scottish or Scandinavian sounding names — how did Pomona, the largest island in the group, end up with a Latinate one?

I try a later edition (1967) of Larousse. For Pomone, it adds that she was the bride of the god of Spring. The entry for Vertumne is the same as in the 1908 edition.

Apart from Graves's *Greek Myths*, which is of no help since Vertumne and Pomone appear to be of Roman origin, there's no dictionary of mythology on my shelf. On the off chance, I look through the indexes of Edgar Wind's *Pagan Mysteries in the Renaissance* and Jean Seznec's *The Survival of the Pagan Gods* but find nothing helpful. Then I try a one-volume, 1927 abridgement of *The Golden Bough*. The closest Frazer comes is a references to the "Pomos of California," an Indian tribe who are mentioned in a chapter on "public scapegoats." Every seven years, this tribe celebrated (and maybe still do, though it seems extremely unlikely — must look up the Pomos, who gave Pomona its name?) "an expulsion of devils." According to Frazer, some 20 or 30 men would dress up as devils, complete with "vessels of pitch on their heads." They would secretly withdraw to the nearby mountains and then descend on the settlement, with the pitch flaming and "all the frightful accessories of noise, motion, and costume which the savage mind can devise in representation of demons." Women and children fled, the men huddled fearfully in a circle. Eventually their courage returns and they drive off the "devils" in a mock battle.

Is this looking-up anything more than an excuse to put off writing? Anything other than a way for me to fill another page with a minimum of effort? Well, I would like to think that all these details will eventually be put to use, that I'll weave them into some brilliant text that if not Joycean might aspire at least to the dense allusionism of John Barth, William Gaddis or any other of those mid-century novelists people used to take so seriously. But to achieve that I'd have to be attempting to create a work of literary art, not simply accumulating some casual observations about a dozen-plus items that happen to be within sight or within reach of where I sit.

5. I start leafing through this book (actually, it's more of a pamphlet), trying to remember why I was going to include it in this list. On page 25 (out of 56) I find a passage that might be the one which inspired me. But first, let me identify this entry: the book is titled *Patti Smith: High on Rebellion*. It was published in Manchester, England. There's no publication date, but I'll guess it came out in 1979. I bought it last year (1996) for $2.50 at a bookstore on West Broadway.

The lines that may have struck me come from a reprinted interview (from *Interview*) with Smith in 1973. The interviewer asks Patti how she overcame her earlier hero worship. The poet (at that point Smith had not yet become known as a singer) responded:

"I once did a show at MOMA, a documentary on getting my knee tattooed by this girl Vali. She's an Italian beatnik-witch and she was a big hero of mine when I was fourteen. She lived on the Left Bank, the supreme beatnik chick — thick, red hair and big black eyes, black beatnik sweaters, and trench coats. Before Edie Sedgwick, she was my heroine. I had pictures of her all over my walls. I never considered her as a real person. I was confronted with the real girl, and I thought, 'oh man, what am I going to do,' because I had dealt with the image for so long. She came over to me and we played all these, not really lesbian games, but like flirting with a boy in high school. When she tattooed me, it was painful. It looks like a little lightning bolt. This girl was real. My photos had become real, and I had to deal with it as a reality. It was a great turning point in my life because it had come full circle. It had begun as an image and then it manifested itself in flesh and blood. She left right after that. She permanently marked me, not only as an image but physically. Permanently branded me. It was something that I absolutely had to deal with for the first time in my life. Right after that I focused in on myself. I turned the flashlight onto my brain, instead of having a searchlight out for Brian Jones, Edie Sedgwick, Keith Richard or Anita Pallenberg. . . ."

When I read that passage it was late at night. I was alone, since E. was on a long trip to Italy. I recalled a movie I'd noticed at the video store, a documentary on Vali. I decided I'd rent it the next day.

The film is not very good. It follows Vali's life somewhere on the Italian coast (Amalfi?). She lives in an isolated house and wanders around being weird in late-'60s style while local men ogle her. The sound is bad, the camera work uninspired. There's been no thought put into the film, apart from the notion of Vali's eccentric lifestyle would be "cool" to record on film.

But then, as I'm watching the film with my hand poised to reach for the remote and hit "stop" and "rewind," I experience a moment of recognition. The Vali of this embarrassing documentary, the Vali who gave Patti Smith a tattoo is the same person who turns up in Ed van der Elsken's *Love on the Left Bank*, a book of quasi-documentary photographs on late '50s bohemian life in Paris. (Was it from these photographs that Patti Smith formed her image of Vali as the "supreme beatnik chick"?)

Although she is a "star" of van der Elsken's book, Vali doesn't earn a mention in a recent appreciation of *Love on the Left Bank*, which describes how, in those photographs, "anonymous camera subjects step out of hundred-year-old bohemian cliches and become individuals, making demands on the people around them, and on whoever is looking at them."

Later that night (a Sunday), after I've returned the Vali videotape to Evergreen Video, I'm watching a show on public television, a short documentary on an organization called "Artfux" which surreptitiously alters billboards in order to further their radical political cause. I recognize that the strategy they use ("detournement") was invented by those very "anonymous camera subjects" among whom Vali moved almost 40 years ago.

6. Walking through SoHo on my way home from work, I notice two women sitting on chairs they have put on the sidewalk. I look at their faces for a split second, then my eyes move automatically to their bare legs stretched out to absorb the end-of-day sunlight, and then, in the next fraction of a second, I notice two metal receptacles sitting near their feet like a pair of tiny dogs. At the sight of these boxes the world seems to stop, but unfortunately I can't. I feel unable to pause and turn to look back at those metal objects because it would seem as though I were staring at the women's legs. In the second or two it takes me to work this out, I've walked too far away in any case to get a good look even if I did stop and turn around. But it doesn't matter. I've seen enough.

Open on the top, their sides slanted slightly outwards, each of the aluminum boxes measures about 6 inches high, 12 inches long and 5 inches wide. My mother used identical high-sided trays to freeze orange juice and other sweet drinks during the blindingly hot Tucson summers. I probably haven't seen or thought about such trays since 1967, but their image has apparently been waiting in my memory. This chance sighting has activated it, but if it hadn't been a sunny late afternoon, if the women hadn't taken advantage of it by donning shorts and taking chairs out to the sidewalk, if I hadn't been walking along the south side of Prince Street, would I have ever thought again about aluminum boxes? How many other such memories do I carry around? How many will I never have the occasion to reawaken?

The kitchen was to the left of the corridor leading into the house from the front door. I call it a corridor because after the first few feet, the brick wall on the left stopped (on the right it continued) and the house began to open up to whoever was entering it. To reach the kitchen, one had to step up (the house was split level but only slightly so) a few inches and then pass between a louvered closet door (washing machine room) and a grand piano (who alive would still remember the manufacturer?). On a narrow strip of wood-paneled wall between the laundry room/closet and the kitchen hung a group of charms from various countries. There were items to ward off the evil eye from the Middle East, Latin America and Europe. They belonged to my mother.

As I contemplate describing the rest of that house, I think how much simpler it would be to draw a floor plan of the rooms in which I spent my 8th to 13th years. There's an artist in L.A. I read about recently who draws floor plans that correspond to the fictional houses of various '60s and '70s sit-coms. I also think of all those murder mysteries which include helpful diagrams showing the layout of the house where the crime occurred. And I think about how many of my favorite novels include maps, from Butor's *Passing Time* to Perec's *Life: A User's Manual*. Well, this isn't a novel and there is no murder involved, although it was a death — my mother's — which occasioned the move from that house but there's nothing so strange in that, and a floor plan would not really be of any help in establishing what it is I want to establish.

In a novel perhaps it wouldn't matter if the corridor really was a hallway, if the brick wall was described as plaster, if the kitchen was off to the the right instead of the left, if the piano faced the living room and not the entryway and sliding glass doors and so forth. If I do feel compelled to try to get these details right in this little paragraph about to recede from me like those two aluminum trays I saw on Prince Street a few hours ago, it's first of all a way of projecting myself back into the world of 2039 East Juanita Street. If I can remember these myriad details and set them down on the page, maybe I will also be able to remember more fully what it was that happened with those walls and within me. Do I believe that there is some magic value inherent in an accurate statement, in rescuing a piece of the past, however trivial it might seem? Are facts set down truthfully like those charms that my mother hung on that narrow strip of light toned, knotty wood paneling? Do they mysteriously resist the force of an external world which would bend our destiny to its often vengeful, malevolent narratives?

7. The seventh of my "things" is also the third that takes the form of a publication from the late 1970s. This is not the result of any plan. These things are being selected the way an inexperienced painter might choose a color, that is, by criteria which fall somewhere between the hunch and sheer randomness.

In contrast to the *Downtown Review* [thing #4], this magazine, a French publication called *art present* (numéro 8, printemps 1979) is full of well-known names. I remember that the friend who gave it to me had gotten to know one of the editors and thought it would be interesting for me to get in touch with him. I never did, having at the time little interest in writing for an art magazine, let alone one in French. It would take seven years before I set off on the path of becoming an art critic. What's interesting to me about this magazine is that it was a kind of harbinger, a clue to my future destiny. I can measure time and how my life changed by looking at the names in its pages. At the time, they meant little or nothing to me, but now I can go through them and say, "I know that one, I've written about this one, I've been to that one's summer house, I hate the paintings of this one. . ." I know this sounds like a rather petty way of measuring my life. No doubt a better way would be to track down my old friend and trade news of our lives since the year in which we shared two sexual experiences and one car crash.

"More than images and relics gathered by the artist from the spiritual beyond, it's a construction in which the spectator, after simply perceiving the work itself, must recover it in such a way that he no longer confronts an object but places himself-as-me, elsewhere, in such a way that this denuded presence is the world and the substance of the artistic experience."

This is written by "the one I know" (a playwright) about two artists (a filmmaker and a composer), one of whom is the one to whose summer house I've been. Prior to appearing in *art present*, the text was published, the credits tell me, in the very magazine in which, seven years after my friend gave me this copy of numéro 8, printemps 1979, I began to write about art myself.

Although I'm astounded by these minor coincidences, I don't expect anyone else to be. Noting their presence here is just a matter of extruding material from my brain and hoping that in the process something illuminating will present itself.

I wander into an alternative space in SoHo and find an exhibition devoted to the history of an avant-garde theater company that flourished in the '70s and early '80s. There's a videotape of a 1979 production I remember seeing in the company's 23rd Street theater soon after I moved to New York. It's a shock to see a film of the play after so many years. There are elements I'd forgotten about completely, such as the continuous playing of Kraftwerk's album, *ManMachineMusic* and references to Ulrike Meinhof. Also striking is a quotation from Kafka: "Nobody could fight his way through here, least of all one with a message from a dead man." (In the play it shows up on the bottom of pie plate — the pie is thrown at an actor playing Andy Warhol.) That quote is so familiar. I've come across it recently but I can't remember where. In a text by Derrida? A play by Richard Foreman? An installation by Joseph Kosuth? I watch the video to the end and leave, a little dazed.

It takes me a year to understand that my shock came out of the fact that I had thought of the play as an ephemeral event which would only have existence (for me) via memory. As each year would pass, I knew I would remember less (which is true, since I'd forgotten about Kraftwerk and Ulrike Meinhof). There would be fewer people around who would recognize the name Squat Theater, fewer who might have gone to see *Andy Warhol's Last Love*, as the play was called. But now, after having wandered into that show (and had a year to think about it), I realize that my memory was not the only thing I had to rely on, that the event is preserved by other means, and much better means, at that. Which can only indicate that it's time to turn back to that which I am sure survives only in me.

(Perhaps writers should be divided into two types: those who seek to write about only what is shared in common — by members of their nation, their race, their generation) and those who write about the things only they know and which will vanish unless they succeed in their task. The latter modify Hemingway's motto "Write what you know" to read "Write what only you know.")

Here's another 14-line poem (no better, and probably worse, than the others):

"Eight Days Post Mortem"

The troubles of a book include
being held in the hand of a legendary rock-and-roll poet
as she stands at the bedside of an even more legendary
and just expired non rock-and-roll poet who was its author.
The troubles of a book are also the joys of the book
she now writes a poem about.
In the poem she describes the book as the only one of
  the 785,000 copies in existence
that was present at the vigil held over the body of its author,
and how she subsequently wrapped it in a Tibetan scarf
which I and a thousand others crowded into St. Marks
can't help noticing hanging from a pocket of her shabby jacket
as she reads the poem about the book she is once again holding,
When she finishes reading the poem about the book,
she picks up a guitar and accompanies herself on Hank
  Williams's "I'm So Lonesome I Could Cry."

8. A book whose title can be translated into English as *Ornament of an Interior Death*. It was published in 1938 and this copy is inscribed by the author to someone named Hubert with a 1946 date. (I translate: "To dear Hubert, who didn't have to wait as long for my friendship as for the book.") I bought it during a visit to Lyon about four years ago for 25 francs (roughly 5 dollars). The pages, some of which remain uncut, are separating from the binding. The cover has a few small stains. Until quite recently, I knew almost nothing about the author, except that he was the addressee of an obscure text (a poem in the form of a letter, published in 1952) that meant a lot to me. Then, last year, I came across his name in a book about Picasso and Dora Maar in which he's described as a poet who was "homosexual, good-looking but weak." The author continues: "Having inherited independent means, he wrote an occasional verse, read, saw his friends, his psychoanalyst and mused upon the emptiness of his life. For some reason, the result of an obscure hurt or disappointment in youth, he was incapable of forming any deep attachment yet suffered from loneliness. He subjected himself nonetheless to occasional protracted periods of solitude in remote, inhospitable places. His poetry was without distinction, but he did not attempt other forms of literary work." The author mentions his own "unsatisfactory" affair with the unhappy fellow.

I wonder if this is an accurate characterization, and have no way of finding out. The most I could do would be to read my 25-franc find. Or I could ask the author of that 1952 poem-letter addressed to Théo Leger. That wouldn't be easy. I could hardly say, is it true that your friend Théo was spoiled, untalented, cold-hearted queer?

Finally my curiosity gets the better of my bibliophilia. As I cut the pages of *Ornement de la Mort Interieure*, using an old brass letter opener decorated with hunting motifs that someone once gave my father, I think how "cher Hubert" seems never to have read the book that was so warmly inscribed to him in May 1946, eight years after its publication. By the time I finish carefully slitting open the leaves of the 106-page book, 52 years after the author penned his inscription, it's in even worse shape than before, with several signatures now completely detached from the binding. The delicate task completed, four years or so after buying the book, I'm faced with a major question: to read or not to read. One thing that would impel me to read it would be the possibility of finding some reference to the author of that 1952 poem-letter. But in 1938, he would have been about 18 and unlikely to be already turning up in other people's poems.

Should I stop writing and take the disintegrating volume over to the couch to read it? While pondering this, I turn to page 14. Actually, because of the title pages, dedication ("à Charles Plisnier") etc., it's only the second page of text. I translate:

> No more birds, the trees make no sound nor the springs
> but this very soft fire which stirs up the wind, it's death
> which is on the move
> and is going to take a man;
> And that one listens in his soul
> to a voice that enchants him in an unknown mood!

He leaves the road; in the depths of himself he looks
  for lost footpaths
inhales in the wind an odor of sleep and trembles
  like a bitch.
An immense fatigue
an immense clarity rises up in his eyes

I flip through the rest of the book, without finding anything that catches my eye. For all I know, there could be dozens of references to the person I'm curious about, but there's no way for me to know. How could I uncover the history of a 60-year-old book of poems by an obscure foreign author? I'm no literary scholar, and, anyway, this may be the kind of thing that escapes literary history altogether anyway.

So much knowledge vanishes with each death. Is literature a way to fill in those empty spaces? Or is it simply a way of trying to make sure that some small part of our memory and consciousness does not similarly slip between the cracks of human history?

What fascinates me about those ghostly figures floating through the back streets and dead-ends of literature: the one-book authors, known only to a small circle; the secondary Surrealists; the forgotten provincial poets of underdeveloped countries? Is it that I identify with them, know myself also to be drifting, ineluctably, into a minor identity? Or is it that the fragmentary, oblique nature of their oeuvres presents none of the daunting challenge of their great, more ambitious contemporaries?

Skirting oblivion is a dangerous game, but no doubt safer than attempting "greatness" and failing miserably.

One evening I go to the Chelsea Hotel to see the work of a painter who died about 10 years ago. (His widow has invited me.) The paintings are pretty interesting if not quite my cup of tea. I suggest another critic who might like to see them and I offer some not very useful advice about galleries. Then, since the studio (seemingly kept as it was when the artist was still alive) in on the second floor, I take the stairs down to the lobby. Jammed onto the wall on a tiny landing is a big painting: a highly stylized, almost caricatured portrait of a woman shown in profile. It has a touch of the psychedelic poster but is perhaps more strongly redolent of tattoo designs. Even in a dingy hotel stairway, it is glaringly bad. Yet I recognize the face right away — it's Patti Smith's "supreme beatnik chick." I search out the date — 1974 — and signature — Vali Myers. Why do images of this woman keep popping up in front of me?

Suppose I'd carefully chosen my "things," instead of impulsively grabbing them. Then these pages could be like one of the projects of the French artist Raymond H.

It's hard to know at first what part of Raymond H's life constitutes his artistic creation. He seems to spend most of his time walking around the city in which he has lived for all his adult life. (Even should he wish to travel, his options are limited because, after years of unpaid taxes, the government refuses to issue him a passport.) Once every so often he'll take a photograph of a facade, a street sign, a construction site. He pays attention to shop windows, occasionally entering a bookstore or a grocery to buy something. He carries his purchases back to his hotel room — for decades he has lived exclusively in hotels, changing establishments as his mood and wallet dictate.

In his room, objects accumulate. He studies them. Certain qualities inspire him to undertake research into their history. He makes notes, he thinks, he embarks on more photography-and-shopping expeditions.

When the time comes for an exhibition — of course our flâneur is an artist, and a fairly well-known one — he delivers to the gallery or museum a selection of his purchases, a few photographs and a title for the work/show. (When the scale of the exhibition permits, he incorporates a piece of the urban landscape such as a street sign or a section of fencing.) The objects and images, he explains to those concerned, are connected by a network of cross-references, verbal and visual puns and private associations. The titles hint, but do no more than that, at the complex of meanings that hold together his work as binding agent hold together a painter's pigments.

I am not selective and methodical like Raymond H. All I can hope for is that through sheer luck there will turn out to have been a thread linking all the persons, places and things whose vectors cross on these pages. Or, if that's not possible, that I manage to produce a rhetorical passage that plausibly unites them. Will either of these things come to pass? It's impossible to say just now, and anyway, it's time for the next thing, number

9. An old map showing part of the coast of northern Spain. It measures about 5 by 8 inches and is glued to a piece of paper slightly larger. There's no date visible but I think it must be 18th century at the latest. The page number (163) and the heading "Description de Biscaye et Gvipiscoa en Enspagne" suggest that it comes from a French atlas. In the style of antique map, the borders (of the maps itself and of the regions it shows) are tinted with colors pale enough to leave the place names legible. The dotted line between "Bifcaia" and "Navarr & pars" is edged in dark yellow on the "Bifcaia" side and pale green on the "Navarr" side. The mountain ranges ("Montes de Occa," etc.) are indicated not by contour lines but by tiny drawings of mountains. These are tinted brown and the water along the coast is marked with a band of dark blue (the rest of the ocean is an etched moiré-like pattern with no color).

Comparing this antique map with a 14-year-old Rand McNally atlas, I can see that the region covered stretches east-west from the Spanish-French border to past Santander and south to a little over halfway between the coast and Zaragoza. It's essentially the Basque country.

Now that I know what the map depicts (though not when it was made), I can proceed to the next question: why did one, or both, of my parents go to the trouble of acquiring and saving it? (The upper right and left corners of the backing paper each have a couple of pin holes. Where did it hang?) Not willing to believe that its presence among their possessions was a matter of mere chance, I examine it for clues. But what am I looking for? I try to find important place names. Pamplona should marked be somewhere but I haven't been able to find it. And also the pass of Roncesvalles, where the battle that inspired the Chanson de Roland was fought.

Glancing at a 37-year-old paperback history of Spain and Portugal (I have a vague notion of trying to figure out the rough date of the map) I see a reference to the kingdom of Navarre (which the map shows at least part of) and I suddenly recall the first movie I remember seeing — *El Cid*. I went with my mother when we were living in Lawrence, Kansas. (Note: look up year *El Cid* was released.)

If the map were of the northwestern corner of Spain instead of the northeastern section, it would be easier for me to imagine why my mother might have had this scrap of antique cartography. Her mother's family, the Ulloas, was originally from that region. But this is not Galicia, it's the Basque country and I can think of no good reason why she would have had it. And of course I don't know whether it was her or my father's or both of theirs, the memento of . . . what?

A souvenir of a visit to the area, perhaps. This reminds me that I still have that stack of my mother's letters from our 1960-61 trip through Europe to finish reading and transcribing. Maybe in one of them there's something about this area of Spain, or even about this very map.

Which reminds me of other geographical questions. What about the Orkneys? And wasn't I going to find out more about Pomona?

Thirty years ago, someone told a little story about a map. It sort of went like this:

The map covers, south to north, from the Black Sea and the Crimea to north of Kiev; east and west, from a line west of Belgorod to the farthest eastern bend of the Don River. It includes the river systems of the Dniester, Bug, Dnieper and Don; the Sea of Azov and northern part of the Black Sea. Many smaller rivers and tributaries are shown and many cities and towns. Military fortifications and camps are marked in red and blue. A good part of Poland is also visible.

Within this expanse, by chance, is the Ukrainian town where my father was born. I can't tell you the name at the moment (I only hope that it's written down somewhere, that some living member of this family remembers), but it's near a city which in less than 20 years will be the site of the world's worst nuclear accident. Does this mean that even if, one day, I decide to "revisit" the place my father left in 1905, I will not be able to? I imagine military checkpoints on the roads leading into the area and a vast, depopulated zone. Do any maps reflect the contaminated state of the land? What color is appropriate to signify fall-out?

That the hand of the map is Russian is certain, from the shape of the ductus and from the fact that when the cartographer writes certain letters in Latin, such as the capital N, he forgets himself and uses the backwards Russian N. (My father never gave up another common Russian reversal, that of holding cigarettes — between thumb and forefinger — with his palm facing his face, instead of turned to the side as is the custom in the West.)

The map was drawn up for the Russian campaign of 1737 against the Turks. (What was my father's family doing at that time? Were they already living in that town the name of which my son can't remember?) In 1737, the region belonged to Poland not Russia. It was called Volhynia and would become the birthplace of the Hasidic movement in a few years. But now brutal gangs of Haidamaks were on the rampage, killing Jews and non-Jews alike. In 1737, Czarina Anna had been on the throne for 7 years (she was 44 and had only another three years of life left to her; the man describing this map had six). In 1737, the Ba'al Shem Tov was 37 and still had 10 years to wait for his great mystical vision.

The Latin "suscoepta" in the title tells us it is an original conception, i.e. not a copy. On the verso are several MS dockets, identifications and press marks, all contemporary.

Why am I telling you this? Because I hope you will be interested enough in the map to buy it. The price is fair, if what I am about to say is true. I have not let any sentimental factors intrude. It doesn't matter the least to me that my father was born in the area covered by the map. After all, I (or my son — there's no difference, now) don't even remember the name of his home town. And even if I did, it may not even be marked on this map.

There's no need to read once again the paragraphs arguing that the initials BK on the lower right hand of the map belonged to a certain Vassily Kiprianov, the "right hand of the first modern professional Russian cartographer Kirilov" and that this made the document "without doubt one of the first modern manuscript maps of southern Russia and the Ukraine." There's no need to follow the allusions to Delisle's Atlas Russicus of 1745 or Kirilov's quarrel with the empress or what Leo Bagrow wrote in Imago Mundi II, pp 78-82, because, in the end, no one will have enough faith in the attribution to pay $6,500 in 1967 dollars. So the map will remain unsold and I will not return to the town which my son will only be able to identify as being near a city where a terrible nuclear accident occurred a dozen years after my death.

10. I can almost flip through the magazine's 36 pages in the time it takes my screen saver (currently "curves and colors") to activate. This issue is dated "Summer 1981" — I've finally escaped from the '70s, barely — and originally sold for $2.00.

At the top of the white cover is the title, *Real Life Magazine*, in black letters and just underneath, slightly off-center, a black-and-white photographic image of Brigitte Bardot. (Was this why I bought the magazine?) Inside there's an interview with B.B. (reprinted and translated from *Le Monde*) in which she comes off as

— a homespun philosopher

"All people work for anymore is money, there's no pleasure in creativity, everything's done in a spirit of self-interest, and the interest is limited."

— a pompous twit

"When I turn a page — in the movies, or after a love affair — I never look back. . . . Being concerned about animals isn't work, it's almost a ministry."

— a reactionary

"There were times when life was beautiful, but because of simple things. We didn't go off looking for complicated stuff, drugs or tropical sects. . . . New Orleans jazz and the Charleston were like fireworks. Now music isn't so much music as noise."

The last lines of the interview remind me of something I came upon about the same time as I bought this magazine. B.B. says "My days are never the same, otherwise I'd not be able to go on living. I'd turn into a machine." This is platitudinous. But the filmmaker Jean Eustache was hardly being so when he told an interviewer: "If I knew what it was that I wanted, I wouldn't wake up in the morning to make films. I'd do nothing. I'd try to live without doing — or producing — anything."

The issue also contains a "Symposium on Post-Modernism," an artist's appreciation of the English pop group Bow Wow Wow, an article called "The Artist as Adolescent," a portfolio of six young German sculptors, none of whom I've heard of since, an interview with a young filmmaker, a pseudonymous art review written in the voice of an elderly Jewish woman from Eastern Europe, an artist's statement (also about Post-Modernism), another artist's statement that I can't be bothered to read enough of to figure out its subject, and, returning to the milieu of the opening article, a lyrical description of Jean-Paul Belmondo translated from French.

As I was wondering if I could find anything interesting to say about *Real Life Magazine* (I couldn't), it came to me that "*14 Things*" is itself a little like a magazine in which one article follows another. What if I published these pages as a magazine? What if I started a magazine called *14 Things*, each issue of which would be devoted to 14 things chosen by the editor (or guest editor)?

One night in 1982 I was standing at the bar of a small basement nightclub on the fringes of North Beach in San Francisco. The d.j. was French, the hat check girl was French, the waitress was French and the decor — white stuccoed walls, lots of arches, banquettes — seemed to me very "Riviera circa 1966," as if waiting for Sagan or Bardot to make their entrance. I was on my second scotch-and-soda when I noticed the girl standing next to me. She was of medium height, blonde, wearing a tight, low-cut black dress. She was pretty, with a touch of smudged glamour that would have recalled to me the young Simone Signoret, if I'd been aware of Signoret.

I thought furiously about how to start a conversation. I no longer remember on what pretext we finally did begin to speak (probably I heard her European accent and asked her where she was from) nor what we spoke about over the loud music. After a half dozen shouted exchanges there was a lull. We turned away from each other and I looked at the bartender, a genial (American) guy who would die later that year in a motorcycle accident, when I suddenly felt a pair of lips of my cheek and then a tongue moving up towards my cheekbone. The lips withdrew and I turned to my left. She looked at me, smiling, without indicating in any way that something unusual had just happened.

I didn't know what to say. I think I stupidly tried to continue our conversation, but at least I didn't ask her why she'd just kissed me. Perhaps a minute had gone by when she began to kiss me again (I write "kiss" but it was really more of an impassioned licking.) She stopped for a moment, then leaned towards me again, this time to my neck. Her teeth grabbed a piece of my flesh and bit hard. I couldn't do anything, pulling away would have just made it worse. She loosened her bite and fell against me. I held her, but she pushed me away. All this was happening in the midst of a crowd, most of whom I knew, and most of whom I was sure were watching me. (They were, as I discovered over the next few weeks as friends recounted the incident from numerous vantage points.) I wanted to get away from the bar, into a darker part of the club. I asked if she wanted to dance. She nodded yes and we went to the dance floor. We began more or less normally, then her strange passion returned and she put her arms around my neck and threw her legs around my waist. This, or variations of it, went on for a while until I got her to follow me to one of the soft banquettes in the back of the club. I don't remember what happened after that. I only know that by the end of the night I had learned her name and nationality and met the girl she had come with. I think I had expected, not unreasonably, that we would go somewhere and spend the night together, but in the end I found a cab for her and her friend, having written down the number of where they were staying. When I got home I saw a deep red mark on my neck where she had bitten me and went to bed happy.

I called them the next day and we arranged to meet. We ended up spending the next few days together, the three of us. We went out to restaurants, walked across Golden Gate Bridge, even returned to the club. There was never any follow up to the passionate (and, I concluded, drunken) advances of the first night, nor even any allusion to them. It had simply been how we met, nothing more than that. Before they left we exchanged addresses and I received two postcards from Zurich (they were Swiss). I had told them that I would soon visit them in Zurich, but eight years passed before I made it there. I never even answered the postcards. I think I didn't appreciate how unusual the whole thing was, how rare. I suppose that I imagined it was the beginning of a new, wildly exciting period of my life where strange pretty girls would always be licking and kissing me in public.

It wasn't, and now those days seem nothing more than an occasion to write stories like this, something to turn to when the common motives for writing have fallen away but I am still spurred on by ambition and guilt, desire and fear. In this case what makes me write is a couple of pages I saw last night in an old art magazine at a friend's house. It was an interview with Julian Schnabel from 1975, years before his career took off. There were a couple of indistinct photographs and Schnabel talked mostly about dogs. When I came home I was desperately wishing that my life had a before and after like his and somehow this led me to think about that Swiss girl and want to write about her. Not because it promised a great short story nor because it had anything remotely to do with Julian Schnabel, but rather because I wanted someone, even if it was only me and even if it was only for an hour, to be able to look at my past with a touch of amazement. I wanted there to appear a disjunction between now and then, between the image of me as I am now and what I was like before, before I even knew I'd become different, even if that difference was not to be the most famous painter of my generation.

11. a kachina doll. It's about 10 inches high. The feathers on its head might have once made it taller but now they have collapsed into a somewhat ratty looking mass on the side.

Where do I start? I've never tried to describe a kachina doll before. Should I try to give the overall impression this one makes or just start somewhere (the head) and describe what I see?

If I remember correctly, the single "ear" coming out from the left side means it's a female deity, but I can't quite bring myself to refer to it as "she."

Like most kachina dolls, the body is compact, blocky and tense, like a football player. But this one is also somewhat elongated. The arms are held to the sides with the two hands pointing forward from the hips. The stance is reminiscent of a gunfighter's. How odd that the first two analogies I make in describing this kachina are to classic images of non-native American violence.

The cylindrical head seems slightly too big for the body. As well as the "ear," a circular protuberance that tapers outward so that viewed from straight on it looks like a orangish-red fan, there is also a nose in the form of an inch-long black cylinder with, painted on each side, a rectangle the same orangish red as the ear but with a white border. If I turn the kachina sideways (it doesn't balance very well on its orange feet, a bit lighter in color that the ear and nose rectangles), I can see the design on the side of the ear: concentric circles of yellow, orange and blue separated by thin black lines which themselves are decorated with regularly spaced white dots.

(At this point, readers who don't care for highly detailed descriptions might wish to skip to #11, but perhaps they already have.)

The head is divided into left (pale yellow vertical rectangle with smaller black horizontal rectangle for eye) and right (blue vertical rectangle with smaller black horizontal rectangle for eye). A thin line borders each of the larger rectangles (blue around the yellow, red around the blue). The background is black (in fact, the black rectangular eyes are simply where the background has been allowed to show through), but three vertical white marks (like the upper section of an exclamation mark) divide the two halves.

The head is separated from the torso by a thick collar of pistachio green.

The torso is mostly orangish-red, but lighter in hue than both the ear and the feet. Its design incorporates pale yellow and blue elements that echo the colors of the head. A turquoise necklace has been painted on the chest, somewhat crudely. The forearms again use the same yellow and blue, colors which are also employed for the bands of color on the kachina's legs between the orange boots and the skirt. The pale yellow and blue colors I've described keep reversing sides:

face:	yellow/blue
shoulders:	blue/yellow
forearms:	yellow/blue
legs:	blue/yellow

The skirt swells out like the walls of that famous Taos church. Unlike the rest of the kachina, its design is asymmetrical. Two thirds of the skirt are white (except for a narrow blue and black border at the bottom). A white-on-black zig-zag pattern marks the division between the white (which is the white of a rough stone, very different from the bright "exclamation" markings on the face) and a complex black, white, orange and blue geometric pattern that may be meant to represent a sash hanging from the figure's waist. Except for absence of the necklace, the back more or less repeats the front.

Let's review the "story" so far:

1. an anonymous painting of a man in his study
2. a painting by my father titled *Habbakuk* (n.d.)
3. a postcard of a painting titled *Vertumme et Pomone* (1710-1720) by Jean Ranc
4. the Fall/Winter 1979/80 issue of *The Downtown Review*
5. a copy of a book called *Patti Smith: High on Rebellion* (n.d.)
6. two metal receptacles seen on Prince Street
7. the printemps 1979 issue of *art present*
8. a copy of *Ornament of an Interior Death* (1938) inscribed by the author
9. an old map of the Basque region of Spain
10. the summer 1981 issue of *Real Life Magazine*
11. a kachina doll

One way to categorize these things:
3 art magazines from circa 1980
3 objects that once belonged to my parents
2 books I've bought recently
1 object seen in the street
1 postcard
1 thrift-store painting

they could also be categorized like this:
3 paintings (one in reproduction)
5 books or magazines
1 map
1 sculpture
1 pair of kitchen implements

or by country of origin:
U.S. (6)
France (4) (includes map of Spain)
U.K. (1) (book on Patti Smith)

by decade (question mark indicates I'm guessing):
1980s (1) *Real Life*
1970s (3) *Downtown Review*, Patti Smith book, art present

1950s (3) thrift store painting? kachina doll? metal receptacles?
1940s (1) Habbakuk
1930s (1) *Ornament of an Interior Death*
18th century (2) (postcard of Vertumme et Pomone, map)

Obviously, I have the mentality of a collector — I am a collector (of books and art as well as written descriptions of things), but there is something I don't like about this mania for acquisition. For instance, it can sometimes stand in the way of my writing. (Is this text an attempt to prove otherwise? and does it?) One item in the preceding list of 11 objects offers a model of how to collect without being burdened by objects and ownership. Can you guess which one? Number 6, of course: the two metal receptacles I saw on Prince Street which reminded me of similar objects my mother had used to freeze orange juice.

Reading an essay on Kurt Schwitters a few minutes ago, I registered how he would comb the streets of Hannover for odds and ends to use in his collages and thought of making a text based not on objects I own but on those I possess only visually, only fleetingly. "Things Seen in the Street," it could be titled.

I still haven't gotten around to finding out more about Vertumme and Pomone, but reading about the meaning of the kachina in Hopi religion (one of their roles is to facilitate the harvest), I thought that the subjects in Ranc's painting are a kind of European kachina. Interestingly enough, the colors Ranc employs — orange, yellow, white and blue — almost identical to those of the kachina I just described (chosen more or less at random from 20 hanging on the wall).

In the book of Habakkuk, the prophet who is speaking promises that even were God to fail in providing the stuff of life, the speaker's belief would be no less:

"Although the fig tree shall not blossom, neither shall fruit be in the vines; the labors of the olive shall fail, and the fields shall yield no meat; the flock shall be cut off from the fold, and there shall be no herd in the stalls:

Yet I will rejoice in the Lord, I will joy in the God of my salvation."

What is the attitude of the Hopis when their harvests fail?

Is my suspicion of my own collecting a residue of the Jewish prohibition of "graven images"? In #2 I contemplate, admire and take esthetic pleasure in the image of a holy spirit when the religion I was brought up in is emphatically opposed to such creations. Did Rabbi G. appreciate the irony of naming a work of art for the book of the bible which says:

"What profiteth the graven image that the maker thereof hath graven it; the molten image, and a teacher of lies, that the maker of his work trusteth therein, to make dumb idols?

Woe unto him that saith to the wood, Awake; to the dumb stone, Arise, it shall teach! Behold, it is laid over with gold and silver, and there is no breath at all in the midst of it."

Actually, the censorious attitude of Habakkuk — "Woe unto him that giveth his neighbor drink, that puttest thy bottle to him, and makest him drunken also" — reminds me of nothing so much as B.B.'s 1981 railing against modern life:

"We didn't go off looking for complicated stuff, drugs or tropical sects."

And couldn't we see her rejection of a film career as a protest against the "graven image"? As a French philosopher (or an American imitator of one) might put it:

B.B. is an iconoclast and the icon she destroyed was precisely the one she herself embodied.

Is it now time to read *Ornament of an Interior Death* from beginning to end, that is, to prove to myself that I am not a mere collector of books but someone who actually cares about what they contain, and is able to do something with it?

Or is it time to look up the year *El Cid* was released and try to figure out why one or both of my parents would have had a map of Northeastern Spain?

Or is it time to attempt to recover who and what I was circa 1980 when I was reading magazines like *The Downtown Review*, *Real Life* and *art present*?

Or is it time to follow the memories awakened by that pair of metal receptacles on Prince Street, hoping to recover the mysteries of my parents' lives and marriage?

No, all that, and so much more, will still have to wait because the only thing it's time for now is number

12. a hand-painted wooden box. It measures about 4 by 7 by 1 inches and is covered with figures in a landscape. Like the kachina, it's been around most of my life but this is the first time I've ever looked at it closely.

The landscape is strange in that it has no horizon line. Some of the figures are standing on floating green islands shaped like long cigars. Others are in brown, canoe-like boats. A few colorful birds hover in the air. In addition to the large islands and the boats, a number of much smaller floating islands, sometimes with grassy plants, strengthens the impression of a watery world. Every detail has been painted with great care. You can see the brushstrokes that make each blade of grass, each tree frond.

I know there's a newspaper clipping inside the box that would probably help in this description but I made myself promise that I won't open the box and read the clipping until I've finished describing the exterior as well as I can.

The background is off-white (about the color of the kachina's skirt) and somewhat discolored. The paint is chipped away at one of the corners. The box is obviously not very new. The sense of age is enhanced by the old-fashioned costumes of the figures, although it is probably not as old as they are. On the largest island on the top of the box, two ladies in crinoline dresses are being attended by a man on a black horse and a peasant bearing a basket of fruit on his head. Although the clothing of the figures is detailed, their faces are blank, featureless. All one can determine is the color of their skin. The complexion of the two crinoline-dressed women is light, that of the horseman (who wears a large sombrero-style hat which he touches with one hand) very slightly darker and that of the peasant much darker. The skin tones range from pink to brown. One lady has turned her head toward the rider, the other extends a hand toward the passing peasant (a male).

On a smaller island another well-dressed woman is attended by two peasants (one male, one female). Two other peasant figures obviously meant to be "Indian maidens," row a boat loaded with green fruit (watermelon, perhaps). A larger boat, propelled by a dark man (like all the male peasants he is dressed in white shirt and pants and an orange vest) with a long pole, carries one woman and a figure which might be a priest of some sort (perhaps a cardinal, given his red garments).

Similar scenes adorn three sides of the box. The back and bottom are unpainted.

Now, I open the box. The interior is painted blood red — a surprise. A thin piece of wood divides the box into two compartments. It has a floral pattern (red roses) painted on its top edge. On the inside of the box's top is a signature and a place:

Corona
Mexico

I next unfold the yellowed newspaper clipping which is lying in the right hand compartment. It's from the *Arizona Daily Star* and is dated Sunday, Sept. 11, 1955 (a little less than two months after I was born).

Most of the clipping is occupied by a photograph of a bald man putting the finishing touches to a group of figures painted on the side of a piano. He is obviously the same person who painted the box. The article reads:

Latest Works Of Painter Salvador Corona
Salvador Corona, former bullfighter who 30 years ago converted a hobby into a profitable profession as a painter, touches up one of his latest works — that of decorating a piano with figures of his native Mexico. The painting is actually a series of figures depicting a sequence of events begun by an invitation to a ball from Carlotta and Maximilian, Mexico's royal rulers during the Napoleonic era. The piano has been on display at McWorter's music store on E. Broadway. (Wong-Sheaffer photo)

Now I fold up the clipping, glancing at the other side to see if there was anything interesting that had been randomly preserved (nothing much) and replace it in the box, which I close and, as soon as I have turned off the computer, for it is 10 PM this Thursday night in August,

1997, and I have written enough for this session, I will replace it on the shelf where it generally resides.

El Cid was released in 1961, which means that I was probably 6 when my mother took me to see it at a movie theater in downtown Lawrence, Kansas. It's the first movie I remember seeing and what, now, is most abiding about the memory is the size of the images on the screen, the mounted knights were as big as mountains. And I recall the seriousness with which the names of the separate kingdoms of Spain (Navarre, etc.) were evoked. I also remember very specifically that it was my mother who took me, that it was something the two of us did by ourselves, without my father.

Things that at one time I considered including but decided against:

— The June 1987 edition of a Spanish cultural magazine called *Sur Expres*. An article titled "Rock-Ola: Algo mas que un club" about a then recently defunct Madrid night spot to which I'd never been inspired this selection — inexplicably.

— Another magazine, *Block*, a radical British review of esthetics. This is the Winter 1986/87 issue and, again, I have no idea what intrigued me about it. Was it Dick Hebdige's "Report on the Western Front: Postmodernism and the Politics of Style"? Terry Smith's "A State of Seeing, Unsighted: Notes on the Visual in Nazi War Culture"?

— A old-fashioned letter opener, made of brass I think, its handle and blade decorated with hunting scenes (this is what I used to cut the pages of *Ornament of an Interior Death*).

— An antique key.

— A dinner plate that I believe was originally the property of Emperor Maximillian of Mexico.

Objects, things — as Ponge says, they "annihilate me." Writing is the opposite of a thing. Sometimes it is devoted to things, but isn't that a mistake? When there are other methods for taking account of things, why should writing waste its time on them, time stolen from the task it is more uniquely suited to: taking account of the immaterial world?

But writing is also a thing or, rather, it is continually crossing and recrossing the border between things and non-things. Every word (and every text, for that matter) is an object, a thing, that we can observe, but it also trails behind itself an invisible cloud of history and associations.

Excuse me, I know this is one of those quaint, 20th-century problems that no one in their right mind still considers seriously. My only excuse is that these pages, these things, all lead away from the present in some way.

I think of a sentence
and how it would echo another sentence
and because I hate the second sentence
I don't write the first sentence.

In an essay on "Freud and Collecting" I find: "No Jew can make a collection of material objects without knowing that these are profanities, false gods, marks of the alien cultures outside the mental and physical space granted to the Chosen People."

I don't believe this.

Does this confirm that I am not a Jew? Not a Jew because my mother was not Jewish. But didn't that ritual bath I took (overseen by a dusty rabbi in little building attached to an Orthodox synagogue on Tucson Blvd. circa 1967) compensate for my mother's non-Jewishness? I think it may have, but I'm afraid I've lost the rabbinical document attesting to the fact. Should I make that missing document thing #13? Can a missing thing be a thing? Isn't the fact that its existence is purely mental and speculative enough to exclude it from the realm of things?

Is one of my points to "avoid passing judgment," as a painter recently said to me apropos of his 30-foot long painting that included 207 panels each drawn from a different source, from Saturday morning cartoons to late Picasso? No, I only have 14 things, not 207, and the source is the intimacy of my own home and history, not that vast marketplace of images that is our culture.

I could say, however, that one aim is to "avoid drawing conclusions."

What conclusions should I draw from that fact? That I introduce a thing into a text when the text threatens to lead me into some difficult territory? No, if anything I attempting the opposite — using objects to approach things I might otherwise turn away from.

I live in fear of being asked to tell a story. Is this why I write about things? The next thing, I have decided, must be something not (no longer) in my possession.

A month has gone by as I've tried to decide on a next "thing" and found myself unable to choose. Each of the possibilities that occur to me, whether it's in my possession or not, has some fatal defect: too personal, not personal enough, too similar to a previous entry, too hard to describe, too obviously full of significance. Perhaps this means that I've lost interest in this project and should stop at 12. This is tempting, but I won't let myself give up.

The problem is that I'm now stranded between the random choice and the considered one. I can neither let myself blindly select one of the items surrounding me and hope for the best, nor can I attempt, through deliberation and instinct, to find the ideal objects with which to conclude this catalogue of some things in my life circa 1997.

One moment I think I've found part of the solution: I'll describe an object which I've seen in a movie. Looking through a book about one of my favorite, talismanic films, I stop at a frame still showing a record player that the characters use to listen to long, melancholy LPs. The image reminds me of canvas from a German artist's series of paintings about the death of some '70s terrorists: a blurry police photo of a portable record player used to smuggle a pistol into a prison. The relationship is intriguing but, unfortunately, the associations raised by these images have nothing to do with these pages.

Then I think of two postcards I have somewhere. Both show the Xocalo in Mexico City. Taken perhaps 30 seconds apart, the photographs (which date from the 1930s or '40s) are fascinating (to me, at least) because they have inadvertently recorded a fraction of a long lost Mexican day. With a magnifying glass, I can note the progress of people and cars from one side of the square to another and also see how other figures remain in place. It's easy to start to make up stories about them, or at least it would be if I could find the postcards. The day I discovered their temporal relationship, I put them in an envelope and labeled it "two Mexican postcards taken seconds apart." But where did I put it? Should the last two entries be things that I've lost?

In the months that I've dawdled over completing this text, the person whom I considered asking about the author of *Ornament of an Interior Death* has died (aged around 70 I think, of a heart attack). This leads me to think about the title of thing #8 as itself a description of an object. What is a collected, treasured, sentimental object related to one's past if not an "ornament of an interior death"?

In the meantime (which, it often seems, is the sotto voce theme of every page I write), I flip through 30-year-old issues of a respected literary review, not reading the unreadable stories and poems the appearance of which no doubt once thrilled their authors, just as I would be thrilled today by an appearance in that same review, and bitterly relishing the tragic ineffectuality of what is still readable. Three decades is long enough for over half of the contributors to have died, for nearly that many to have sunk back into the oblivion from which they probably believed they had emerged, and for a few pages to have slipped through into some kind of survival.

I must have something better to do. I do, and this is it. I'll read whatever it takes, from yellowing copies of the *Paris Review* to 10-year-old articles about defunct nightclubs written in languages I don't really speak to all the preceding pages that still refuse to tell me how, with what two objects, I should bring an end to this exercise.

I remember when television stations would "close down" for the night with the national anthem played over an image of a waving American flag. Somehow, I can imagine this whole text as the spoken commentary to an unchanging image of a test pattern.

In the meantime, let me go back to number 12 again, to that box hand-painted by Salvador Corona, or rather not to the box but to the piano mentioned in the newspaper clipping that I found inside the box, to the subject of the painting on the side of the piano: the "sequence of events begun by an invitation to a ball from Carlotta and Maximilian, Mexico's royal rulers during the Napoleonic era." Could it have been this one:

"Mexico had never seen a ball on such a scale. The decorations were superb. The ballroom, a converted patio hung with tapestries and flags and banners, was lit by forty-eight crystal chandeliers. The supper was a triumph of French gastronomic art; the fireworks, on which Mexicans delight, provided a fantastic display of French pyrotechnic skill; there was unlimited champagne for all. The Imperial couple, who had driven from the palace escorted by a detachment of French cavalry, arrived at nine o-clock, the Emperor opening the ball with the daughter of the municipal Prefect and the Empress with General Bazaine, and did not leave until one in the morning." (Joan Haslip, *The Crown of Mexico*, 1971)

What might the sequence of events in Corona's painting have been?

If one turned left after the piano, went a few feet, stepped up the few inches that separated the level of the entryway and the rest of the house, one would have been in the living room, and on one's left would have been a large, built-in bookcase, half of which was given over to volumes relating to Maximillian and Carlotta. Somewhere else in the house, or perhaps in a bank safe deposit box, was other related material: china plates with the imperial coat of arms, a pistol with a similar mark, various military decorations, a diamond brooch said to have been the Empress's.

Will the accumulation of points ever result in a full portrait? If so, it will take many more than 14. Maybe I'm hesitating because the next number is supposed to bring bad luck? Could that be it? Suppose I skip the thirteenth thing, as some elevators "skip" the thirteenth floor.

13. First names:

Francisco
Vicenta
Santiago
Francisca
Clemente
Maxima
Atiliano

Maria
Pedro
Jesus Maria
Dolores
Consuelo

James
Charles
Maria
Archibald
Isabelle
George

Josef
Klara
Meyer
Rosa
Henry
Dorothy
Joseph

Last names:

Ulloa
Montalro
Muñoz
Martinez
Hernandez
Alvarez

Howatt
McDonald
Perceval

Rubinstein
Dvorzak
Weisberg
Moskovitz

I look at the names, now entered into my computer. They have been transferred from the blue-paper-and-ballpoint-pen document that my mother once went to the trouble of drawing up so that one day I would be able to consult it as I am now doing.

But to what end? Why have I separated the names, divorced not only husbands from wives but even first names from last? Is it a way of affirming that genealogy is meaningless? But I don't believe it is. Or is it simply because it helps me to imagine these ancestors, about many of whom I know nothing? "Francisco Ulloa" or "Klara Dvorzak" or "Charles Howatt" are less suggestive than: Francisco, Klara, Charles. I can think of them as young people, growing up, falling in love, producing offspring.

And at the same time, these single names are distinguished from the double name ("Raphael Rubinstein") with which I will sign this text and which will remain indivisible from it (or so I hope).

No one will ever read this family tree with the emotions that I bring to it, but these pages in which I have inserted the names of some of my ancestors do not require any special relationship from the reader. On the contrary, all of the foregoing is designed expressly for readers who have no connection to the author.

How much connection do all of the foregoing "things" have with one another? Do I care about their interrelationships? Evidently, but not in such a way that I seek out items for the sake of their connectedness, though neither do I resist affinities.

These pages have not been structured like a piece of music or like a building. If they resemble anything, it's simply a walk from point A to point B, a short journey marked by a series of encounters whose interrelations are dependent only upon the instinct that has guided the choice of route.

I know that if push comes to shove I can find something to say about absolutely any object that I choose to place in front of myself, but I would also like to find an object about which I have nothing to say, a thing which I will feel is sufficient unto itself, that will supply a point at which I can satisfactorily bring to a halt this erratic walk.

I pick up a book about a saint, a sculptor and a poet. It happened to be the topmost volume on a stack of books sitting next to me. Is it time for something which doesn't pertain, or at least not in any obvious way? I know I could never find an object full enough of symbolic importance to occupy the concluding position of this catalogue, or if by some miracle of concentration I did, I'm sure I'd have no wish to write about it.

Have you ever noticed how when someone tells you of a book that you "absolutely have to read," there develops a kind of mental block against even opening it? (What's particularly strange about this phenomenon is that generally it only occurs between friends and acquaintances; if a newspaper reviewer or literary pundit recommends a book, we're much more likely to act on the suggestion.) I think that something similar is happening here. If I decide to pay attention to a certain object (rather than selecting one more or less at random), it's as if I'm making a suggestion to myself that I immediately start to resist. And maybe, perverse though it sounds, this is all to the good. What, after all, is more boring than selecting some significant item and proceeding to write about its significance? (Note: formulate a theory of the oblique?)

It's not that I don't want to find connections — that's the unstated (until now) aim of these pages — and it's not that I don't want to penetrate to the heart of things. It's just that, gazing out the window at the endless New-Jersey-bound traffic, listening to the sublime grooves Augustus Pablo laid down 20-plus years ago in a Kingston, Jamaica, recording studio on a street called North Parade, I'm still willing to defer that direct confrontation whose style I am still not able to master.

I'm already making plans for the next text I'll write. Maybe "plans" is too concrete sounding for something still so vague. I dream of writing something as different as possible from "14 Things" but I know how unlikely that is. Already, from a manila envelope labeled "faits divers" I'm pouring a stack of newspaper clippings onto my desk. Could these form the basis for another text? Perhaps, but I suddenly find that I'm in the mood for throwing things away. Into the wastebasket, then, go half of the envelope's contents, including:

"Pope Says the Devil Actually Exists," *San Francsico Chronicle*, Nov. 16, 1972. I don't know why I've held on to this since I have no particular interest in either the Pope or the Devil. As a teenager I collected amusing headlines and this might have been a late addition to that collection. More interesting is the other side of the clipping which has a photo of Angela Davis with her vast Afro halo alongside one Billy Dean Smith who, the story says, had just been acquitted of two "fragging" murders in Viet Nam.

"Rutgers Re-examines Dispute Over Nazism," Dec. 18, 1986, *New York Times*, an article about an investigation into the 1935 firing of a professor whose anti-Nazi views clashed with the political view of the then head of the German department. The professor is 81 and went on to teach at City College, while his Nazi-sympathzier boss died in 1978 in Germany. The article says that a recent investigation of the incident found that politics was not the cause for the professor's firing.

"Spanish town ends its 100-year war'" from an English-language paper published in Palma, Mallorca, about the town of Lijar which had declared war on France in October, 1883, because Spain's King Alfonso XII had been "insulted, stoned and cravenly offended by a French rabble" while traveling through Paris the month before. There's no date on the clipping but it's probably safe to assume that it was published sometime in October, 1983.

I toss into my "sell or give away" box a copy of a Belgian art magazine from 1990 and wonder why I can't bring myself to get rid of those copies of *The Downtown Review*, *Real Life* and *art present* or, at the very least, *Sur Expres* and *Block*.

I tell myself: Get rid of all things that do not pertain to you personally. I also tell myself: Do what is necessary so that the things around you acquire pertinence to you and your life.

When I was 17, I inherited a large house full of objects that pertained to my father. Instantly, all them now pertained to me. It took many years to physically and mentally sort through those things, a few of which made it into these pages.

a room reflected in the glass doors of an old cabinet
a feeling of contentment with no obvious cause
a nighttime summer thunderstorm
a glance that I'm not sure you notice which says:
I am aware that this is one of the days of our lives
nostalgia for when I first arrived in New York

and lived with fewer books and the feeling that eventually
  I'd read all of them
the words that would ribbon themselves around this night
will not appear until later, on another night
lines that keep measuring the distance between me
and the page, the page and the street, our two bodies
waiting for one measurement to slip
and try to match itself to something
that stretches in another dimension

The last item comes from the same folder ("Family") as the one preceding it:

14. a birth certificate. It's on legal-size paper. Printed in an arc of upper-case letters across the top is "Estado de Guanajuato" and underneath this a vignetted engraving of the Mexican national emblem, an eagle with a snake in its beak. The eagle is perched on a cactus and extending out from the cactus is an array of rifles, bayonets, canon, spears. Draped over the spears are what I take to be flags. A pyramid of small canon balls and a pair of crossed pistols rest on the ground. There's also a kind of stony plateau underneath this assemblage and, along the bottom edge of the image, a decorative border of ribbon and plants. A pattern of horizontal lines indicate the horizon and clouds billowing above it.

Underneath this etched image is a printed line (I will now begin translating everything into English):

"Year of 1912, Worth 50 centavos"

Then the main text begins. It is typewritten in blue ink — or has the ink merely faded to blue? (Topic for research: what color of typewriter ribbon was used for official documents in Mexico circa 1912?) One of the documents peculiarities is that every number or date is given in both numerical and written out form.

"Registered 188 one hundred eighty and eight bis. Without rights. Howatt Elia. In the city of Guanajuato, Thursday 3 three of October of 1912 nine-teenth hundred and twelve, a 12:30 twelve thirty AM, before me the Judge of the civil state Jesus Gasca, appears Senor Pedro Ulloa, residing at 9 nine calle de Desterrados, 54 fifty four years old, married, miner who says: that Monday 23 twenty three of this September, at 6 six in the afternoon, in the same house, was born a baby girl who appeared alive and who took the name ELIA; and that she is his grand-child and legitimate daughter of Senor Jorge A. Howatt from Tyron, Prince Edward Island, Canada, 39 thirty nine years old, married, miner and of Senora Maria de los Dolores Ulloa, from Santa Ana and this vicinity, 28 twenty eight years old, married; that the paternal grandparents were Senor Archibaldo Mc. D. Howatt finado and Senora Isabelle Howatt who are alive and the maternal grandmother Senora Maria Jesus Hernandez also living. Witnesses were Senores Miguel Dominguez, living at Zangarro de la Cruz Blanca, 54 fifty four years of age, married, tailor and Alfonso Garcia, residing at calle de Pocitos letra S. 22 twenty two years of age, single, privately employed."

Then follows a few lines of legalese and a reference to something called "the law of foreignness" by which Senor Howatt retains his English nationality. The only signature on the typed document is the Judge's, and he wraps his name in an oval flourish.

I have so many documents that pertain more closely to me than this 85-year-old birth certificate of an aunt I never met — Elia Howatt died Jan 27, 1915, aged two years, three months. My mother was born the day after and given a name, Consuelo, in the hope that her birth would be a consolation for the loss of Elia. Why, then, is it this one to which I devote an hour or so on this Saturday evening in mid-November in my 42nd forty second year?

If I had a similar certificate for my mother, perhaps I'd have transcribed that. Or perhaps not.

I try to picture the scene at the writing of this document. An official room of some kind in the Guanajuato city hall. The Judge in a suit. Does he wear glasses? And the four men: two miners, a tailor and the young "empleado particular" (I translated this above as "private employee" but in truth I'm not sure what it means). Was Elia's mother also present? Did the men dress up for the event? At 12:30 on a Thursday afternoon, they were probably on their lunch break so perhaps weren't able to change into anything fancy. What was the relation between the father and grandfather and the two witnesses? It's interesting that although Pedro and George are identified as "miners," the witnesses practice other professions. Perhaps it was too difficult for their miner friends to get to city hall from the mine which was a ways outside of town (that much I know), so they called upon two men who worked closer to city hall.

The father is 11 years older than his wife, and only 15 years younger than his father-in-law. The father-in-law is the author of a sonnet I translated somewhere near the beginning of these pages. How did it go?

"Why"

Why do you weep as you write? Your letter
has marks of burning tears
which without doubt will fall on the page
like a magnificent string of diamonds.

Now ungrateful luck separates us,
but don't cry anymore, lovely one, I beg you;
Eventually, bliss and peace will arrive
in this life satiated with wounds.

Together some day, no more apart,
your sorrows will be illusory myths
and love will bring us constant joys

If you return to crying for necessary sorrows,
dry your loving tears
with the infinite kisses of my lips.

Could the death of Elia be one of the "wounds" that "satiate" life? It's possible, I suppose. Now, looking at the names I transcribed in number 13, I wonder if the subject of "Why" was Pedro's wife Jesus Maria or, what is more likely, the woman (absent in the family tree from which I earlier drew names) with whom he had an illegitimate family in a nearby town. But that's another story, one that would need some other "thing," on some other day, to make me find a way of telling it.

I've finally gone through my mother's 1960-61 letters from Europe to see if I could find any clue about the map of Northeastern Spain. In a typed letter dated Feb. 13, 1961, I found a passage which convinces me that the map was hers:

". . . . From Madrid we drove to Burgos and stayed overnight. It is a lovely town and I'd liked to have stayed a week. The church is one of the most beautiful I've ever seen, at least on the outside. The cathedral in Barcelona is the most wonderful on the inside. I didn't go near a church in Madrid. The religious atmosphere in Spain is really oppressive. It is certainly pleasanter and more natural in France. The next day we drove to Bilbao. I've always wanted to go there. It is very ugly, nothing old, smoky and dingy, but I just loved it, mostly because it is full of Basques. We had ttoro (fish soup) and chacoli, which is a dry bitter wine, and ate centollo, which is a huge crab. I heard several people speaking basque. 99% of the men wear berets. They are entirely different from the rest of the Spaniards. Many people are shabby, but almost no one destitute like the ones in the south. I'd liked to have stayed there too, and hope someday I get back. I hoped I'd see some dancing or singing, but they all said they were too busy in the winters, and only have time in August. The next day we drove to Bayonne. . ."

It's 5:30 pm on a Saturday in mid-December. The sky is already dark. I listen to the insect-like buzz of my computer and, from across the loft, the hum of the space heater and recall reading somewhere how all or, at any rate, most machines produce a sound that is equivalent to a B-flat note. As abruptly as I began, I'm finished with "14 Things," I guess, although the preceding pages seem, as I try to think about them, worrisomely amorphous and provisional. Oh, well.